Harlequin Romances

OTHER
Harlequin Romances
by GLORIA BEVAN

Many of these titles are available at your local bookseller
or through the Harlequin Reader Service.

For a free catalogue listing all available Harlequin Romances,
send your name and address to:

HARLEQUIN READER SERVICE,
M.P.O. Box 707, Niagara Falls, N.Y. 14302
Canadian address: Stratford, Ontario, Canada N5A 6W4

or use order coupon at back of books.

Bachelor Territory

by

GLORIA BEVAN

Harlequin Books

TORONTO • LONDON • NEW YORK • AMSTERDAM • SYDNEY • WINNIPEG

Original hardcover edition published in 1977
by Mills & Boon Limited

ISBN 0-373-02073-2

Harlequin edition published June 1977

Printed in U.S.A.

CHAPTER ONE

ALISON swung her blue Mini off the main northern New Zealand highway, turning into a long straight broken by clumps of tall cabbage trees that looked as though it would go on for ever. At the turn-off she had left behind the busy city-bound traffic and now there was only the empty road with green farmlands on either side and beyond the hazy blue of distant hills. Presently she was following the course of a swiftly-flowing river, discoloured with soil washed down from the hills of the hinterland and bordered with raupo and blowing flax. At intervals along the route corrugated iron sheds with notices of kumeras for sale flashed into view. Then she was driving over a long bridge spanning the river, pulling into a bay to allow a great stock transporter with its double row of tightly-packed sheep to thunder past. Ahead she glimpsed the scattered buildings of a small town. So this was Dargaville, the northern river town with its history of gum-digging and its Yugoslav settlers. She moved slowly along the quiet street, taking in the white stone buildings of an earlier era, the rambling Colonial-style timber hotel with its red iron roof and shady verandahs under which was parked a line of dust-smeared Land-Rovers. No doubt, she mused the Yugoslav names on the stores were a legacy from early settlers who a century ago had made their long journey by sailing ship to a new and unknown land to wrest a living digging gum from the giant kauri trees covering steep bush-clad hillsides. There was, however, nothing out of date about the stock in the stores, for the tastefully arranged show windows displayed a variety of late model goods ranging from farming equipment and fishing gear to fashion garments and exquisitely crafted furniture.

A brief pause at a small clean shop for coffee and sand-

5

wiches, then she headed the Mini towards a petrol station on a corner of a side street. As she waited for the attendant to appear from inside the building her gaze lifted idly to a painted sign swinging overhead: HAERI MAI. KAKASE. Everyone knew that the Maori word meant 'welcome', but the Yugoslav word was unfamiliar. All at once she became aware of the attendant, a thin youth with unruly fair hair and a shy grin who was eyeing her with frank interest. Alison, however, was accustomed to meeting that particular expression in masculine eyes and took little notice. It was a reactionary thing—her hair, that bright mop of coppery-red curling strands that sunlight turned to living flame and no amount of vigorous brushing could subdue.

'Will you fill the tank, please?'

'Sure, sure.' But he continued to stand motionless, gazing in her direction. At last he moved towards the pump and picked up the hose. 'Staying long in Dargaville?'

'No, I'm just touring around the north, having a look around.'

His face fell. It would have been too much to hope for, a girl like this staying right here in town. A girl with that open eager look about her face and crisp copper-coloured curls that made you want to run your fingers through them.

In an effort to divert his attention she indicated the sign above her head. 'Kakase—that's a new word to me. It's Yugoslav, isn't it?'

'That's right.' It was a feminine voice who answered and Alison swung around in surprise to meet the smiling gaze of a tall well-built girl in T-shirt and jeans who had paused beside the car. Dark eyes, long black hair caught severely back from her forehead, a sleepy-eyed smile. Alison liked her from the start.

'I know a little of the language,' the stranger was saying, 'enough to know that word means "welcome".' She had a low pleasant voice with a smile in it. 'It's the first two words that get me puzzled.'

6

'That's easy,' Alison told her. '*Haeri Mai* means "welcome" too, in Maori.'

'So that's it! I guessed it must be Dargaville's way of saying "Hi". I've only just arrived here myself—going far?'

Alison was watching the needle flickering on the dial of the petrol pump. 'I don't know yet. I'm heading out towards the coast, having a look-see.'

'Me too.'

For the first time Alison noticed the canvas hiker's pack lying at the other girl's feet.

'I'm touring the district too,' the stranger was saying.

'Could I give you a lift between here and there?'

'Oh, would you! She smiled with warm friendliness. 'I was hoping you'd ask me. I may as well come clean and tell you that's the reason I followed you in here. You don't mind, do you?' The slow smile broke across her face once again. 'I only arrived in Auckland from London a few days ago by air and I'm hitch-hiking my way north. So if you've got a seat to spare——'

'Hop in!' Alison leaned across to throw open the passenger door, then made to shift the bags to the back seat.

'Don't bother, I'm used to travelling steerage.'

'Not this time,' Alison said firmly, and tossed her bags to the rear of the car. She paid the attendant and slipped the car into gear. 'Right, we're on our way!' She guided the blue Mini out towards the main street and soon they were running through the town.

'I'm Mary, Mary Vasanovich——'

'Alison.'

In no time at all it seemed they were through the shopping area and making their way into suburban areas where the wide streets were lined with homes of an earlier era, each one surrounded by lush green lawns and bright with flower borders.

'Mmm, smell those roses!' The dark-haired girl sniffed appreciatively as they swept past an archway festooned with great blooms of Shot Silk. They were entering a newer

7

part of the town where modern timber bungalows painted in rainbow shades of pastel blue, salmon pink, lilac and lemon shone in the sunlight. Each house was set well back from the roadway and spreading lawns swept down to the street. A wealth of blossom was everywhere, carnations, stock, petunias. 'Hey, look up there!'

Alison's glance swept up the green slopes at the roadside where the white timbers of an old misson house glimmered amongst clustered native trees. Evidently the building was now the local museum, for on the hillside lay a long open boat all of sixty feet in length.

'It's a carved Maori canoe,' Alison explained. 'The early Maoris usually used to build them of totara timber, carve the prow with their primitive stone adzes, then hide the canoes from enemy tribes in swamps and rivers. This one was probably dug up from one of the lakes around the district. The canoes still turn up occasionally from some swamp or river bank, even these days—tell me, how did you get on hitch-hiking up from Auckland?'

A smile tugged at the corners of the other girl's wide mouth. 'I didn't set out to hitch-hike. I got forced into it. Actually,' she confided laughingly, 'it turned out to be more of a pick-up.'

'How come?'

'Well, you see, I started off from the city on a motor scooter. I'm used to travelling that way at home and I thought it would be fun to pick up a cheap used scooter while I was in the city and then make my way north that way. Fun! I must have been out of my cotton-pickin' mind!'

'It wasn't?' Alison's eyes were on the road ahead.

'Not for long, not really. English roads are a whole lot different from these winding highways, for one thing. I hadn't allowed for the northern route being one sharp bend after another, up steep hills and down again, and it's just too bad if the big trucks almost shave you off as they pass. I could have coped with that, though, but half way up the steepest slope of all, bang, the motor scooter gave up the

8

struggle. I tried and tried to get it started again—no way! Then just when I was wondering what on earth I could do with the thing myself, along came this knight of the road——'

'Don't tell me, let me guess!' Alison guided the car past stockyards at the roadside, swept on between long lines of macracarpa pines. 'He was driving a big American car with oodles of power——'

Mary's dark eyes were twinkling. 'Better than that!'

'Big English car, then, driven by a guy with nice manners, English tailored clothes?'

'Guess again! The American limousines and the English luxury jobs were the ones that passed me by and left me standing there on the road with that great useless lump of metal. I was just about giving up, wondering how long it would take me to push that flipping thing up the mountainous slope, when along came my rescuer, a huge Maori man with a big smile driving a brewery delivery van.'

Alison laughed. 'Did he put you and the scooter in the back of the truck?'

'Did he ever! He had a couple of his mates in the front with him and he told me if I didn't mind going in the back of the truck with the casks he could take me and the scooter. I jumped at the offer! He was wearing a black work singlet and you should have seen his shoulder muscles! He picked up that scooter as though it was a kid's toy and tossed it into the back of the truck, then he heaved me in after it. He even dropped that heap of metal at the local garage here in Dargaville for repair.' Mary's low voice held a chuckle. 'It was worth putting up with the remarks hurled at me whenever we stopped at one of those funny little settlements along the road.'

'I can imagine. Cheers, calls, miming, shouts of "Have one on me!"'

'How did you guess?'

They were out in the country now with no farmhouses in sight. Mile after mile with only the green sheep-dotted hills

9

on either side, and a fragment of road ahead as they climbed towards a cloud-filled sky.

A few miles further and they had left even the scattered farmhouses behind. Now they were sweeping up clay banks where there was nothing in sight but the vast sheep-dotted hills with their long boundaries of macrocarpa pines, the black steers grazing in valleys far below. All at once the smooth surface of the highway gave way to rough metal, and loose stones thudded against the undercarriage of the car.

Mary broke the silence. 'Actually,' she confided, 'Grandfather Vasanovich gave me this trip out to New Zealand as a birthday gift. He insisted on providing me with spending money too. Wasn't it good of him? I mean, a trip isn't much fun without something to spend.'

'An overseas trip half way around the world,' Alison marvelled. 'How lucky can you get?'

'Oh, it has a few strings to it.'

Alison taking a hairpin bend swerved sharply to avoid a pile of red clay that had broken away from the cliff above and subsided over the greater part of the roadway. 'Such as?'

'I'm supposed to be on a sort of mission. There's something I'm supposed to look up or come across or ferret out somewhere in this part of the world and take back home with me when I go. Not that I think there's a chance of it turning up. Out this way, on the road to the coast and the sandhills, happens to be my starting point to begin operations—Help!' Mary drew in her breath sharply as a small one-way timber bridge loomed ahead and a silver milk tanker bore down on them. Alison, however, had braked to a stop and the next moment the driver, with a friendly salute, swept past, leaving a cloud of dust in his wake.

Alison asked curiously, 'But whatever could you find up here? Not even fossilised gum that the place was famous for once. That's all been worked out years and years ago.'

'Aha, you'd be surprised! How about a husband? Preferably one with a Yugoslav name! Oh, Grandfather didn't spell it out, but I've got a sneaky suspicion that was his whole idea in sending me out here. In a way I don't blame him for trying. Failing the husband it seems he's depending on me to bring him back some news of his long-lost relatives who he thinks might still be living somewhere about these parts. That part of the plan he's quite open about. Guess you'll know that Vasanovich is a Yugoslav name,' she went on, 'but I'm really three-quarters English. Grandfather emigrated to England when he was a young man. He married an English girl and he's stayed there ever since. His only son was my father who died when I was a baby, so I never knew him, or my mother either, come to that. Anyway it seems that Grandfather had a brother who left the family home at about the same time, but he went even further afield, out to the wilds of New Zealand, and from what I can gather it was wild in those days. From what Grandfather told me all you needed then to make a living in the country was a tent and a pick axe so you could collect the fossilised gum from the huge trees that grew all over the hills. Kauris, they called them, didn't they?'

Alison, changing gear to take the steep slope rising above, nodded. 'There are still a few trees left down in the gullies. See, down there——' She gestured with her hand. 'The tall leafy trees with the straight trunks heading for the sky non-stop. In those days, so they tell me, kauri gum was worth real money. Those shops in the main street of Dargaville with their Yugoslav names—I expect they would be the descendants of the pioneering stock.' She slanted Mary a teasing glance. 'You're one of them yourself, almost.'

'Could be. Grandfather's really keen on the ancestor-bit, though I've got a feeling he'd be even more interested in the idea of a modern guy with a Yugoslav background as husband material for his only grandchild. What a hope! As to those long-lost relatives, heaven only knows if I'll have any success when it comes to tracing them. It would be a different story if there had been any correspondence to refer to, but there's been nothing to go on except an old letter. Not much to go on, is it? And Grandfather hasn't even got the letter. He just has this vague idea there was one that

11

came years and years ago from a place in the north of New Zealand called Dargaville, but it was all so long ago. It would be awfully lucky if anyone of that name happened to be living up this way.'

'Oh, I don't know,' Alison flashed Mary a smile. 'Who knows? This trip might be lucky for you! Might even bring you a Yugoslav husband, maybe, with the name of Babich or Simich—something like that.'

'Now you're talking like Grandfather—am I boring you to tears with all the family history, or rather, the lack of it?'

'No, no, go on. So you're out in New Zealand with the idea of looking up your family connections?'

'You could put it that way. Oh, there was one other thing, what really sparked off the whole enquiry, I expect—a report by an old crony of Grandfather's who had been out in this country on a tour. He happened to mention that somewhere on his travels through the north of this island he'd noticed the name Vasanovich on a gatepost. He couldn't remember which gatepost, which town, only that it was somewhere out towards the coast after the tour bus had left Dargaville. But all that was five years ago. Not much to work on, is it? All the same, it's nice having a tour around the district and,' Mary smiled her slow smile, 'it's fun looking.'

After a moment she went on, 'Grandfather knows I've always been crazy about foreign travel and evidently he decided to kill two birds with the one projectile, bless his scheming old heart! So here I am!' She gave a low chuckle. 'The old boy doesn't dream that I'm on to what his real idea is behind all this overseas trip he's given me, or that I happen to know what this locality is famous for. Can't you guess?'

'Kumeras,' said Alison promptly. 'It's kumera country and that's for sure. All the way along the road today I've been passing big storage sheds with notices, kumeras for sale. You must have noticed them.'

'Kumeras?' Mary stared across at her. 'What on earth are they?'

12

'A sort of sweet potato. The early Maoris were the first ones to grow them. Guess they hadn't much else to live on except birds they managed to snare, fish and seafoods and the odd fern-root. The district must have the perfect soil conditions for growing them, because now it seems like the whole population is busy producing them for the city markets.'

Mary burst out laughing. 'Well, anyway, you're wrong! It's bachelors!'

'Bachelors!' Alison echoed blankly.

'It's true! Seems the district around here is full of them. They're working on farms, living in huts on their own or else they're partners in homesteads and holdings and farms with other single guys. They're living on their own, coping with cooking and cleaning and household chores, at least I hope they are, just waiting for the right girl to walk in.' Mary gave her crinkly-eyed smile, 'or drive in at the front gate. Grandfather's old crony was a bit hazy about the Vasanovich bit, but he was downright certain of the bachelor part of his story. Said he'd run into them all over the place. The way he put it was that the district around here was lousy with them, all wanting wives.'

'You mean,' Alison slanted her a teasing glance, 'they're desperately wanting a cleaning woman or live-in cook.'

'Don't be so unromantic! Don't you believe in ... love?'

'Love?' Alison laughed her clear young laugh with the catch in the throat. 'What's that? From all I gather after listening to my friends it's something that's highly over-rated, especially after you've been married for a year or two.'

'Married friends? You?' Mary looked astonished. 'But you're only about seventeen.'

Alison pulled a face. 'Twenty,' she corrected promptly, 'all but. I just look this way. It's maddening, but there's nothing I can do about it. It comes of having a young face and a mop of silly babyish curls.'

'Twenty,' Mary marvelled, 'and you've never been in love? The real thing, I mean, sweep-you-off-your-feet, don't-care-about-a-thing-else-in-the-world variety. I just don't believe it! Hasn't there been *anyone*?'

Alison laughed. She changed gear and they swept up between high hills where arum lilies grew wild on cleared green slopes. 'Oh, I've had one or two near misses, guys I liked for a while or they liked me, but it didn't last. Maybe I expected too much, maybe they got tired of me. Who knows?'

'Are you telling me you've never met anyone special?' Mary persisted incredulously. 'Any man who stirred you?' Her sideways glance swept over Alison's mobile young face, the short nose and sweetly curved mouth, coppery coloured curls blowing back from a tanned forehead in the breeze.

'Not really.'

Mary's tone was thoughtful. 'You've always lived at home with your parents, in a small town?'

Back where she came from there hadn't been a town, but Alison let it go. 'That's right, in the waybacks, actually. This is my first venture on my own. How did you guess?'

Then why, Mary wondered, the wistful note in Alison's voice, the shadow in the clear hazel eyes? Aloud she said, 'I thought so. There's something about you ... not like a city girl ... more open, somehow——'

'Outspoken, you mean. I'm always getting into trouble because of not stopping to think before I say something awful.'

It seemed, however, that Mary was not to be diverted from her subject. 'Living in the country all your life you must have met young sheep farmers, lots of them?'

Alison's gaze was on the tea-tree shaded bend ahead. 'Practically nothing else but.'

A rural delivery van sped past and when the dust had settled Mary pursued her enquiries. 'And you didn't fall for any of them?'

'Why should I? What's so special about the breed?'

'What's so special? I'll tell you something. Back in England where I come from there's a sort of romantic legend grown up around your young New Zealand sheep farmer.'

14

'You're having me on!'

'No, no, it's true! He's lean and tough and bronzed and strong as they come. A hard worker too. A colourful character who can ride hell for leather over the hills all day and dance all night. And as a lover—a girl only has to look at him once and pow, she's head over heels, overboard fathoms deep!'

Alison laughed. Somehow it was easy to laugh with this companionable girl who in some odd way she felt as though she had known for ages. 'I wouldn't know. I've met swags of sheep farmers, young and old and inbetween, but never one like that except...' She broke off in some confusion— for unbidden, there he was right there in her mind, the dark stranger whose face stayed with her. Young and vital, lean and bronzed with an impression of whipcord strength about him and the look in his eyes of a man accustomed to gazing into far distances. To her chagrin she could feel the pink creeping up her cheeks. 'Well, only once,' she confessed as the silence grew, 'and then I only saw him for a minute.'

'Must have been some man, some minute,' so Mary had caught that betraying tide of colour, 'to make you remember him so clearly.'

Now when it was too late Alison tried for carelessness. 'Just like you said, only more so, I guess.' She attempted to shrug away the masculine picture in her mind, said with studied nonchalance, 'but I never got to know him.'

'Too bad.'

'Not really.' Alison bit back the confidences that trembled on her lips. She *must* remember to heed the warning red light that had clicked on in her mind. And only just in time. From now on she had to check her naturally impulsive outspoken nature and keep her thoughts to herself. 'He was just a man I saw once.' In spite of her resolutions not to give anything away regret tinged her tone. 'I didn't even know his name.'

But you have a pretty good idea! Craig Carter, a name, a man you couldn't ever forget.

15

Mary was saying incredulously, 'You didn't try to see him again?'

'No.' She wondered what her companion would say were she to tell her that she was at the moment running away from that very possibility. See hem again .... unexpectedly something deep inside her said quite clearly and without the slightest quiver of doubt. If only I could!

To change the subject she switched back to their earlier conversation. 'How did you come to know that this was bachelor territory? The beer truck driver?'

'No, not him. It was Grandfather's old crony, the travelling one, who passed on that bit of interesting information. I happened to be there at the time he mentioned it. All those unmarried young farmers and a Yugoslav settlement too in the north of New Zealand was enough to give Grandfather ideas.' The smile was back in Mary's voice. 'Quite a way to go to find a made-to-measure husband, wouldn't you say, but a little thing like distance wouldn't put Grandfather off, not once he'd set his mind on anything. And believe me, he's really set his heart on his one and only grandchild keeping up the family traditions and changing her name to something like Vasanovich, even if it does cost him a couple of thousand dollars to pull it off. I guess,' she said wryly, 'he thinks it's my last chance and for that it's worth taking a risk. Luckily he can afford to please himself. I could have told him, I did actually, that he's throwing his money away, because frankly as a husband-catcher I'm a dead loss, seeing I couldn't come up with one even in England. I mean, you can scarcely count two broken engagements. Anyway, what odds if I am still on my own and haven't met anyone I really care about! When you're pushing thirty it doesn't do to hang on to all those romantic notions. You have to toss them overboard and settle for a life of your own. I've got a good job in a law office, promotion coming up, a cosy little flat—I'd be a fool to throw it all away. I think Grandfather's got an idea I'm a bit lonely, with no husband or children, no relatives except him. What he doesn't seem to be able to get into his dear old head is that there are worse things than loneliness, like getting hitched in marriage to the wrong man. He's too old, I guess, to remember about love. Or could be he's right. Maybe love is just a trap, a delusion that can complicate your life, who knows? After all,' Alison caught a wistful note in the quiet tones, 'you can't have everything.'

'Those two broken engagements,' Alison asked curiously. 'What happened? Or would you rather not talk about it?'

'Oh, I don't mind. It's ages ago now. Funny, things that happened to me when I was nineteen or twenty seem part of another life. It's just me, really. I have this failing, character flaw, whatever, this sickening sentimental trait. I always fall for men who in one way or another manage to get my sympathy. Maybe it's something to do with always having wanted to be a nurse and having been sidetracked into office work. Colin was in a wheelchair when I first met him. He'd been in a terrible car smash that had left him crippled for life. I guess I was sorry for him and that was all, because when the crunch came and the wedding date was only three weeks away I changed my mind about marriage. Everyone thought I was cruel and mean to let him down at the last moment. I suppose I was in a way, but he had no problems financially. He could afford to have someone around to take care of him. It was only at the last minute that I came to my senses and realised our relationship wasn't exactly a love thing, not on my side anyway. Pity, sympathy, yes— but that's not quite the same, is it?'

'I guess not.'

'In those days I thought a lot about love, all that madness you read about in novels. It just never happens to me. I don't know why I'm going on and on about my love life, if you could call it that——'

'You said there was another engagement that didn't work out?'

'Oh yes, Mervyn. Another disaster, actually. I was sorry for him too. You wouldn't think you could make the same mistake all over again, would you! Don't you believe it. I was taken in all over again. I was sorry for Mervyn too, but

17

for different reasons. He'd had a financial crash, lost all his property and assets, his life savings really, and had finished up with having a go at taking his own life as a way out of his difficulties. I suppose I comforted him, bolstered up his flattened ego, and after a while he came to rely on me for everything. It was quite a time,' Mary observed wryly, 'before it hit me that all he wanted was a mother figure. I did him a service when I finished everything between us and gave him the ring back. After that he learned to stand on his own feet again. The last I heard of him he had started up in business again, modestly, but at least it was a new beginning—not wildly exciting romances, are they?'

CHAPTER TWO

THE next moment Mary was cheerful again. 'I'll tell you something. For me this trip out to the other side of the world is the fulfilment of a dream, something I've always longed to do. Guess I've been brought up on tales of that gum-digging ancestor of mine. So when the chance came to make the trip out here I said to myself, why not? Mary Vasanovich, this is your chance to see something of another country. New Zealand, here I come! I was so lucky! The firm where I work gave me three months' leave of absence and their blessing. I do seem to have been going on and on about myself—now tell me about you. You're Alison ——?'

'Car—— Wynyard.' Swiftly she caught herself up, hoping Mary hadn't noticed the slip. She would have to do better than this in future when it came to remembering her unfamiliar name.

'Live at home, you said?'

'I —— used to, until three weeks ago. There's nothing much to tell really.' In spite of the resolute brightness of her tone, her voice faltered. 'I—— lost my parents a while ago ... in an accident.'

'Oh.' For a moment Mary was silent. 'I'm sorry. Tough on you.'

For a moment the sheep-flecked hills merged into a mist of green and Alison blinked the moisture from her eyes. 'I'm all right, most of the time. It was just ... so sudden.' Swiftly she ran on, 'My mother wasn't very strong and Dad ran the farm on his own. I used to help him with the outside work and somehow it was awfully hard to get away for holidays. Now I'm taking a break. I'll have to find myself a job sooner or later, but right now I'm just touring around.'

'All by yourself?'

'I don't mind. There wasn't anyone else I could ask to come along with me.'

'Here's one girl who'd be glad of the chance!' grinned Mary. 'I could go equal shares with you for expenses, petrol and all that. It's up to you—but I just thought I'd ask.'

'Love to have you along.'

'Done!' When Mary smiled her eyes crinkled up and she had a low infectious laugh. Somehow the other girl seemed to Alison to be a good friend to have around. For all Mary's gaiety Alison sensed the other girl's easily-pierced armour, an insecurity Mary tried in vain to cover. *She's alone in the world as I am, but she's brave and resourceful and she won't let circumstances get her down.*

It was merely an offer from a stranger, yet a little of the chill unfamiliar feeling of isolation and being utterly alone in the world was falling away. It was almost as though something deep inside, a hard frozen lump, had begun to melt, as if she were coming alive again. For the first time since the start of the journey she was swept by a feeling of freedom and adventure.

'That's settled, then,' Mary was saying happily. Her gaze lifted from the sombre mass of pine plantations on a hillside they were sweeping past to the road ahead, curving upwards towards a fleecy white cloud on the horizon. 'Where did you say we were heading for?'

'I didn't. I just had this crazy idea I'd like to take a look at the coast. I've never seen this part of the country before, though it's not a great distance from where I come from. Somehow it's always fascinated me, just hearing about it— the great harbour and wild coast with its strong rip and dangerous currents. It seems so remote, way off the tourist route, nothing but sea and farming land and sandhills.' She added laughingly, 'And the wind! No wonder all the homesteads around here have those high shelterbelts of trees around them. This is my second week on the trip. I I spent the first one in Auckland, staying in a motel and lazing on the beaches. It was quite an effort to tear myself away.'

'Where will we put up tonight, do you think?' asked Mary.

'Oh, that's no problem. There's a little tent packed away in the boot of the car. We can put that up if we have to, but if we decide to stay around here for a few days we'd only have to knock at the door of a farmhouse for shelter. They're probably quite used to strangers turning up for a bed away up here in the hills.'

Mary quirked an expressive eyebrow. 'You mean, the bachelor establishments?'

Alison laughed. 'I'd forgotten about them. Failing that we could always go back to a hotel in Dargaville. Let's play it by ear, shall we?'

'Suits me. You didn't plan the trip, then?'

'Plan it? Heavens, no! This time last month I would never have believed I'd be here on the road. It was just——' her voice broke and she blinked the moisture gathering at the back of her eyes. She said huskily, '—the way things happened.'

The way things happened. In the silence the miles fell away. Alison's gaze was fixed on the road winding ahead but her thoughts wandered. Could it be only three weeks since they had brought her the message? Even now she hadn't fully recovered from the shock and horror that had overcome her on learning that both her parents had been killed outright in a head-on collison on the road while returning from a visit to friends a few miles distant.

Not that they were actually her parents, but as good as, far better than. The matter of birth made not the slightest difference to her feelings towards them. How could it? For no flesh-and-blood parents could have been more loving than Jim and Dot Carter.

Indeed, as the years had slipped by she had all but forgotten that although everyone called her Alison Carter her name was actually Alison Wynyard. Funny how she remembered the name of Wynyard, although she had heard it mentioned only on one occasion. That was when, as a child of eight, she had been told by her foster-mother the circumstances of her birth. How Dot Carter had a lifelong friend who had always been closer to her than a sister. The friend had married and gone to live in Sydney, then on learning she was suffering from a terminal illness and having no close relatives of her own, she had written begging Dot to take the baby girl and bring her up as her own child. 'My husband Victor travels all over Australia in his work,' the sick woman had explained, 'so it would be impossible for him to care for her. He agrees with me that you are the one we would like to entrust her to.' So a month before the brave mother passed away the Carters had made a trip to Australia and brought the baby girl home with them to New Zealand. 'And I'm so *glad* we did,' Alison's foster-mother had told her with a close warm hug. It was the best thing that ever happened to Jim and me, having you with us.' Perhaps it was, for the years passed and to their regret no children were ever born to the couple.

Jim Carter, quiet and kindly, was an indulgent father. He adored Alison from the first moment he saw her. He had always intended to arrange a legal adoption for the daughter he loved so dearly, but the years had slipped by without the matter having been attended to, and anyway, what did it matter?

It was the same with the property, the lush green hill paddocks he had broken in from rough scrub country over half a lifetime of hard physical toil. 'It'll all be yours when we go, lass,' he had told Alison often enough. Poor Dad, how horrified he would be were he to be aware that things hadn't turned out that way. It wasn't his fault that fate had taken a hand in events. Such a simple thing to shatter two lives, a truck approaching at speed on the wrong side of the road, a collison on a sharp bend. In a matter of seconds the shining new car of which Dot and Jim had been so proud was a mass of crumpled metal in the dusk. *It wasn't fair.*

It was only later after the funeral that the impact of shock had given way to a chill sense of loss, a feeling of emptiness in the house that was far removed from ordinary periods of absence. This was for ever.

A week later the family lawyer had come out from town to express his sympathy and to explain to Alison her legal position in regard to house and property.

At first she couldn't take in the information the lawyer was trying to get through to her. It was strange how his clipped tones seemed to be coming from a distance even though he was seated right there at the table opposite to her in the shadowy lounge room.

In the absence of a will, he informed her, the estate would pass to the Carters' nearest relative, a nephew living in the South Island, a man of whom Alison had heard of only vaguely and never met. The lawyer, a small neat-looking man of middle age with shrewd grey eyes, allowed himself a moment of compassion for the stricken-looking girl who seemed so alone in the big empty house. The next moment he pulled himself together. 'Your position would of course have been entirely different had there been any legal adoption. I'm afraid your guardian made a big mistake there. I tried to get him to see to it on quite a few occasions over the years, but he always put it off in the same way as he never got around to making a will. I haven't a doubt but that he and his wife fully intended the property to be left entirely to you, but their sudden deaths ... and as the law stands ... a combination of unfortunate circumstances ... I'm afraid——'

'It's all right, I understand. I'm not blaming them.' Alison's voice broke. 'They were wonderful to me. I owe them everything.'

'Not quite everything,' he said with irony. Through the open window his gaze moved over lush green hill paddocks neatly fenced, black steers grazing on the flats below. Hillsides were dotted as thickly as daisies with newly-shorn sheep and in addition to all this there were many hundreds of acres of green productive land, farm machinery and vehicles, not to mention this well-built old homestead. It was too bad. If only Jim Carter had followed legal advice and made a will years ago—but he had always put it off, with the result that his neglect had dealt an irrevocable blow to the girl he had always regarded as a dearly-loved daughter. 'However,' the lawyer cleared his throat and

23

sought to offer what comfort he could, 'I have no doubt that matters can be satisfactorily arranged to your benefit. It is to be hoped that the nephew,' he consulted his papers, 'Craig Carter, will arrange as suitable monetary compensation once he becomes aware of the circumstances. No doubt we could come to some arrangement——'

'No! Please——' Alison's soft lips were set firmly. All at once the thought of haggling over the place that had always been her home was unbearable. This cold calculating discussion concerning the affairs of the two she had loved best in all the world was something she couldn't take. 'I don't want anything from him! I wouldn't dream of accepting it!' She leaned forward, urgency and appeal in her voice. 'You'll tell him, won't you? You'll make it quite clear to him that it's okay, I can look after myself. I don't need to take charity from anyone!'

'Charity!' Mr Black was shocked. 'My dear girl, I don't imagine you fully understand the position your parents' unexpected death has put you in. You'll have nothing. Look at it this way,' he went on in a milder tone, 'isn't it only what Jim and Dot would have wished?'

'*Please* tell him!' It was no use. He could see that her mind was already made up. 'It's time I learned to stand on my own feet,' she summoned up a shaky smile, 'and the sooner the better. Promise you'll tell him exactly what I said.'

He looked at her oddly. 'If you prefer,' he murmured soothingly. Alison thought he was speaking to her as one would to a fractious child.

Shock, he was thinking, she's still in a state of shock. Give her a week or two, then when she gets back to normal she'll see things in a different light. Good lord, she would be a fool to refuse to accept a little financial help after losing what amounted to a sizeable inheritance. Something about this girl touched him. She was so alone, and so damnably independent! It was a combination that didn't augur well for a girl left to her own resources—but then, his trained legal mind flicked back into action, it wasn't likely that she

24

would be on her own for long, not with those looks and that glorious copper-coloured hair. Even now when she was so pale with dark shadows around her eyes she was quite lovely. There was something unconsciously appealing about her. Jim Carter and his wife should have had more forethought, leaving their ward penniless as well as alone!

He jerked his thoughts aside. He couldn't imagine what had come over him, letting himself get involved personally with his client. He must be getting soft. Aloud he said, 'I understand the nephew is the owner of an extensive sheep station in the South Island. It is possible that he may decide to sell out here, in which case——'

'Sell Te-o-nui?' Alison's eyes were distraught. The next moment she pulled herself together. What difference would it make? She wouldn't be here. But Banner would! Her heart gave a stab as she remembered the graceful white mare she had raised from a long-legged foal. No doubt at this moment, she thought forlornly, Banner was no more than an item on one of the long lists of items set down amongst the papers on the table. Just part of the estate along with the stock ponies and the goats who ran wild on the far hills. 'On second thoughts,' anxiety sharpened her tone, 'there is something you could arrange for me with the new owner——'

'Good, good.' Mr Black was endeavouring to hide the note of triumph in his voice, 'I knew you'd come around to seeing things my way.' Picking up a pen, he drew a sheet of paper towards him. 'Now, about the amount involved. I would suggest that under the circumstances you settle for no less than——'

'No, no, not money! I told you, I thought I'd made it clear. It's my horse——'

'Your—horse?' Plainly the lawyer was taken aback.

'Not just a horse,' protested Alison indignantly, 'she's a wonderful mare, a show-jumper! It would tear me apart if Banner went to someone else, some stranger. Do you know I raised her from a tiny foal.' All at once the shadows fled from her face, her voice was animated, eager. 'She's got

25

such a big heart! You wouldn't believe the trophies and ribbons she's won at shows and gymkhanas. I've hunted her for the last three seasons. Oh, I've lots of offers to sell Banner, she's quite well known in riding circles, but I could never part with her. I didn't think,' she said very low, 'I'd ever have to. You'll tell this Craig Carter man——'

'Of course, of course.' Rarely were the lawyer's feelings stirred by professional visits, but there was something about this girl, a fierce independence, a desperate courage, that touched his heart. 'If it would help,' he spoke briskly to hide his unexpected rush of emotion, 'I could make it clear to Carter that the mare means a lot to you and if he's willing to let you have her——'

'Let me have Banner!' Indignation sparked her tone.

'I'm sure there'll be no difficulty about it,' Mr Black said smoothly. 'I'll pass on to him your special request that the animal is not to be sold and that you will come and collect your mount as soon as you have a permanent address.'

'Oh, would you?' Alison's face shone with relief. That was another thing about this girl, the expressions that chased one another across her face. You could tell her feelings at a glance, though she would probably be horrified were she to know that her emotions were there for anyone to read, plain as day. Extraordinary girl ... she had appeared quite unmoved at the loss of an inheritance that should have been hers in the ordinary course of events. Yet here she was blinking away tears over the chance of losing her mare. Just as well he had remained a bachelor. He would never understand women, not in a hundred years.

'But supposing,' her hand flew to her mouth, 'the property is put on the market right away and Banner——'

'Don't worry, my dear.' Could that be himself speaking in that sickeningly father-like tone? 'There's plenty of room on my property to graze your mare. She'll be looked after there if the estate is sold in a hurry and you can come and collect her at your convenience.'

'Thank you, thank you. It wouldn't be for long, a mouth or so. Only ...' bewilderment and worry struggled in her expression. She had no intention of letting either the lawyer or the Carter man have her address. The last thing she wanted was to be pestered with his charity-cheques. Meantime, the man was a sheep farmer, he must know how to care for animals. All at once the solution was plain. She would arrange for a horse transporter to call at Te-o-nui and collect Banner. She wouldn't need to have any contract with Craig Carter. She decided to use her own name from now on. That way he would never find her.

'You'll tell him, won't you, that Banner's a show-jumper, a very special one? He mustn't let anyone else ride her. I'll take her away,' the eager tone faded into indecision, 'one of these days ... before long.'

The lawyer nodded. 'I'll pass on your instructions, don't worry.' He thought again, if only Jim Carter hadn't been such an impractical, obstinate fool. Now this lovely girl found herself out on her ear. No office training either, he suspected, to help her get on her feet. He wouldn't mind betting she had never been away from Te-o-nui in her life. She'd been too busy helping Jim run the place—and what had she got out of it all? Exactly nothing! That nephew had fallen in for an estate worth more money than most folk would get their hands on in a lifetime. It wouldn't hurt him any to make over a lump sum to the girl. *If she would accept it.* Without warning the shaft of pity pierced him once more and silently he cursed the Carters for their happy-go-lucky attitude towards all legal commitments. The girl seated opposite him at the big table seemed so defence-less. It was her eyes that got you, they were so clear and trusting, like a child's. Aloud he said, 'Pity you couldn't have had a word with the man yourself——'

'Oh no!' she cried in alarm, 'I don't want to do that!'

'But he won't be here until next week. I had a word with him on the phone and he's coming up to have a look around and decide what he's going to do. He mentioned something about putting this property and the South Island one on the market and taking up land in the north, but of course he hasn't even seen Te-o-nui yet and he may well change his mind when he gets here. You've made some plans for the future?'

'When I leave here, you mean?' If he were carefully skirting the painful truth she seemed determined to face up to it. 'Oh yes.' That was another lie, and this time she suspected Mr Black was not taken in, although he gave no outward sign.

'You'll be able to cope, then?'

'Oh yes!' Unconsciously she lifted her rounded chin. 'I have a little money of my own, enough to carry me along for a time.' The moment of bravado faded and a shadow darkened her clear-eyed gaze. 'I thought I'd take a holiday and tour around the country for a while. I've never been further north than here. The Mini's my own,' she added hastily. 'Dad gave it to me on my last birthday. Everything else . . .'

'That makes sense,' Mr Black agreed as her voice faded away on a sigh. He gazed around the comfortably furnished room with its deep wing-chairs and long picture windows. 'The place does seem a trifle large for one small young woman.'

The next minute Alison had recovered herself. 'That's what I thought too. I've only got to pack my things,' the bright voice faltered, 'and say goodbye to Banner.' Swiftly she ran on, 'the nearest neighbours, the Gilberts, have been ever so good. They've offered to look after the stock and keep an eye on things until,' she took a deep breath, 'the new owner arrives to take over. They're going to store a few boxes of things I won't need right away, riding gear and all that.'

'And after your holiday? Had you anything in mind, Miss Carter?' So he hadn't believed her after all. 'I understand there's a typist's job coming up in my office shortly, one of the girls is leaving the district. If you've had some business training you might be interested?'

Alison shook her head. 'No, I haven't.' The only training she had was in farm work, helping to dock the lambs, riding and mustering, drafting cattle, ordinary things like that.

Looking at Mr Black's impeccable city suit, his cold grey eyes, she decided it would be useless trying to explain.

For Dot, always delicate and easily tired, had taken no part in the outdoor activities that formed part of the life of the average New Zealand sheep farmer's wife. She preferred listening to the radio, working on her tapestry pictures, reading and knitting. So Alison helped her father with the endless tasks of the seasons and she had loved it all.

'Alison's a home girl,' Dot had often observed contentedly, and she supposed she was in a way. Or could it be merely that she had never had a chance of being anything else? Certainly she enjoyed baking a cake, watching the dough rise for home-made bread, whipping up a batch of feather-light scones to take to the hungry shearing gang down in the shed. But that didn't mean she wouldn't enjoy another type of life, something quite different. She didn't know what exactly, but something.

'I understand that country folk are always on the lookout for domestic help,' Mr Black's unemotional voice cut into her thoughts. 'You would have no problems there. You could even find work in the district if you preferred to stay around here.'

Stay here, to be patronised and pitied by Mr Craig Carter! Mr Black, you've got to be joking! She bit back the angry words, took a deep breath and said quietly, 'No, not here.'

'I understand, and maybe you're right. Personal feelings might get in the way. But there are other places.' He was gathering up papers and placing them neatly in his leather satchel. 'You will be sure to leave me a forwarding address as soon as you've finished your holiday?'

'Oh yes, of course.' But she had not the slightest intention of keeping the promise. Leave an address where the Craig Carter man could send her his charity cheques and handouts, all at the lawyer's suggestion? She could imagine Mr Black's smooth tones. 'Perhaps in view of the circumstances a certain sum set aside for the foster-daughter would be in order? Merely a suggestion, of course, there is no legal obligation.'

Never! She couldn't bear the thought of wrangling over a home that had always stood for love and security. Charity from a strange man was something she didn't have to take. 'I'll let you know.' She wasn't used to lying and was afraid it would show, but apparently Mr Black had his mind on other matters.

'Good. I think that about wraps it up.' The lawyer rose to his feet. 'Perhaps things will work out right after all.'

Privately she reflected that if by working out all right he was referring to her accepting money from a man she had never met she didn't give much for her chances.

'Goodbye, Miss Carter! And good luck!' Even his handshake, Alison thought, was dry and lifeless. She summoned up a smile and accompanied him to the door, watching as he climbed into his dust-smeared car and moved down the long drive towards the road.

She supposed it was a stupid impractical way of looking at things. There was no doubt Mr Black had thought her quite out of her mind to refuse the financial assistance he had offered, but when you came right down to it, it was a handout, made out of pity to a girl who had missed out on her inheritance. Her foster-parents had done more than enough for her, she was quite agreeable for their property to be passed on to one of their own flesh and blood. What she was concerned about was the thought of accepting money from *him*. Nothing would induce her to consider such a thing. She fancied the lawyer had got the message as to her feelings on that subject, but if by some unhappy chance the nephew contrived to communicate with her directly, despite her change of name, she would make the matter plain in no uncertain terms.

Unconsciously she sighed. It didn't help any to stand here at the doorway just looking, not with the grass blowing in the wind, sheep dogs barking, cats frisking around her legs. She only hoped the new owner would look after the animals properly. Oh, what was the use of thinking?

Better start to pack. Tomorrow she would leave here for ever. There was nothing to stay for—now.

In the evening she drove down to the Gilberts' farm taking with her a large carton of clothing and personal possessions which Mrs Gilbert, kind and motherly, had offered to store for her in a spare room. They were so kind, the Gilberts, asking no hurtful questions as to why she was leaving without waiting to greet the new owner. Perhaps they already knew. 'Don't worry about anything back here,' Mrs Gilbert told her. 'Boy'—Alison knew she was referring to the single middle-aged son who lived at home, 'will move up to Te-o-nui tomorrow and stay until the new man comes to take over.' It was nothing, they were only too pleased to be able to do something to help. The unspoken sympathy was comforting and eased some of the sense of loss and emptiness she couldn't seem to shake off.

Next morning she fed the farm animals as usual, then carried her luggage out to the Mini. Her zipped travel bag held summer clothing, shorts, sun-frocks, swim-suits, and in the big cardboard carton she had packed her most precious possession, the Topanti saddle for which she had saved for so long and had sent out from a firm away over in London.

Now there was only one thing left to see to, and that was something that wrenched her heart.

As she moved up the slope Banner caught sight of her and nickered gently, moving towards Alison with her prancing gait, long white tail blowing in the wind. The foolish tears pricked Alison's eyes as she stroked the mare's head. 'You'll be all right,' she whispered against the thick white coat. 'The Gilberts will look after you until *he* comes.' She brushed away the tears with the back of her hand and fled. To look back would only make the parting harder to bear.

Back in the silent house she went through the rooms, satisfying herself that she had left nothing of her own behind, closing the long lounge room picture windows against the threat of fleecy gunmetal clouds hanging low on the horizon. The windows—all at once she froze, looking

31

down a vista of green paddocks to the road below where a long red car was approaching and somehow she just knew it was about to turn in at this entrance. The next moment it did. She watched as a tall masculine figure sprang out of the vehicle to open the gate, drove through the opening and closed the gate behind him. What if he were the new owner arriving earlier than expected to look over his inheritance? He would be bound to be impatient to see over the property he now owned—but he wasn't going to see her, that was for sure! She mustn't let herself be trapped here, forced to meet him, accept his hateful sympathy and worst of all, become involved in sickening arguments concerning the place she had always thought of as home. She couldn't bear it, she wouldn't! She went on peering through the venetian blinds. Thank heaven for slats that permitted her to look out and remain unseen. Now he was driving through the second gateway. Flight for her was out of the question, but maybe she could still avoid a meeting. She would wait in here and hope his inspection would be concentrated on the land and the stock. A sheep farmer himself, he would naturally be interested in the lush paddocks, the newly-shorn sheep and the black beef cattle roaming the slopes. One thing, he was alone, and that meant he hadn't brought his wife along with him to see the property. A woman would be far more inclined to linger in the house and garden. With a little luck plus the help of the floor-length yellow velvet drapes at her side Alison might yet avoid coming into contact with Craig Carter.

She held her breath as the stranger closed the last gate behind him and sped up the winding drive towards the house. Now he had braked to a stop in the driveway and was getting out of the car. She could see him clearly, a tall man, broad-shouldered and younger than she would have expected him to be. My, but he was good-looking in a tough, sun-bronzed sort of way. A typical sheep farmer, slim-hipped with a deceptive leanness. She wouldn't mind betting he could toss a fully grown sheep over a fence and think nothing of it. He was taking his time, glancing around sheep-studded slopes around him, a tall man in beige slacks and navy blue shirt, soft suede shoes, thumbs hooked in the leather belt encircling his hips. Presently he took from the pocket of his shirt 'the makings' and leisurely proceeded to roll himself a cigarette, running the flimsy paper along his lips.

Somehow she couldn't tear her gaze away. Dark hair blowing back from a strong rugged face, a goodhumoured mouth—she could even glimpse the deep cleft in his chin. Now he was gazing towards the house and it seemed impossible that he could remain unaware of her scrutiny, but of course venetian slatted blinds took care of that.

She went on looking, she couldn't help herself. There was something about him that held you, an impression of authority in his stance, a feeling that he was a man to be reckoned with. The sort of man you could be drawn to— she pulled herself together—in other circumstances.

At last, just when she felt she couldn't bear the suspense another minute, he came striding up the concrete path and she heard the small garden gate shut behind him. Swiftly she slid behind the shelter of the curtains. It seemed to her fevered imagination that even his footsteps were firm and decisive. The next moment she heard the door open into the back porch and presently she could hear him moving through the kitchen, going into the passage, opening bedroom doors on either side, then closing them again. Clearly he was giving the house a brief inspection, no more. With luck she'd get away with it! Scarcely daring to breathe, she heard footsteps approaching the loung room and knew he was in the room. Help! He was approaching the window where she was hidden from view. The footsteps stopped and the silence seemed to last for ever. Then the quick decisive steps moved on and Alison let out her breath on a long sigh of relief. It must only have been the view from the picture windows that had attracted him. She was overcome with a wild desire to giggle. What if he had attempted to draw the curtains? Or supposing he had brought a wife with him? She would probably have made a close inspection of the newly-hung gold velvet drapes that had been Dot's pride. At least that was something to be thankful for. Odd that he hadn't brought his wife. Odder still were he to be unmarried, a man like that—she pulled up her thoughts with a jerk.

When she ventured another glance outside he was striding towards the garages and a few moments later he took out the Land Rover. So he intended having a run over the back paddocks? Well, that suited her fine. Once over the brow of the high hill at the back and he would be out of sight of the house. She could slip into the Mini and make her escape long before he had returned from his tour of inspection. Thank heaven he hadn't entered the garage where her car was parked. It would have been awkward had he noticed its absence on his return. Somehow he hadn't looked the sort of man to overlook anything.

It seemed an age until she saw him taking the rise. She took a chance then and slipping out of the back door, hurried across the yard. She was almost at the garage when she saw the Land Rover stop. What if he were returning right away? In a panic she rushed into a nearby shed and in the shadowy rear of the small building, rubbed away the cobwebs from a forgotten window and peered through. For goodness' sake! She stared in amazement, for it was Banner who had captured his attention.

He was standing at the gateway patting the mare's white neck and Banner, traitor that she was, appeared to be enjoying his attention. The next minute he had vaulted the fence and taking an old bridle hanging on the wires, slipped the bit into Banner's mouth. So that was the idea—he was going to take her over the jumps in the paddock and try her out. How dared he ride Banner? Who did he think he was?

Alison watched breathlessly as he set the white mare to the painted rails, each one set a little higher than the last, that Alison had put up herself. Of course Banner took them without a fault. Anger melted away in pride as the mare gathered herself up spread out and sailed effortlessly over

34

the bars. At least he would see what a fantastic show jumper Banner was. He could ride, she admitted grudgingly, and he wouldn't do the mare any harm. He might even keep her in training. He took the mount back over the jumps and again she performed brilliantly. At last, with a parting pat, he let her go free. Surely now, Alison reflected, he would get on with his journey over the hills.

She waited for a few minute, then ventured to push open the door and peer around it. Goody, goody, he was back in the Land Rover, and even as she watched the vehicle vanished over a grassy rise. Now was her chance! In a flash she had run into the garage and was flinging open the door of the small blue car. Luckily she had a brand new battery and the motor started at a touch. Better close the doors behind her so he would notice nothing different. She sped down the winding drive, opening the closing gates with fumbling fingers that shook with haste. Then at last she was out on the quiet road.

Wow-ee! She had made her escape—but only just in time!

Out on the open road her taut nerves relaxed and she slackened speed. There was no point in hurrying away now that the danger was past, 'danger' being one Craig Carter.

All the way to Auckland she couldn't seem to stop thinking of him. No wonder, for unwittingly or not, he had turned her life upside down. Travelling along the northern motorway she reached the city in late afternoon and booked into a clean and quiet hotel within walking distance of the city.

Auckland fascinated her, this essentially outdoor city set between two harbours with its volcanic cones and bushland and seascapes. It's the start of summer, she thought, strolling down Queen Street where the men wore light shirts and walk shorts, the girls summery frocks, and the gay lava-lava of the Pacific islanders from Samoa, Tonga, Cook and Nieu Island, brought gaiety and colour to the main street.

The days slipped by as she explored the city where there were so many places to visit, so many things to see. It

35

would all have been so different had she had someone to see it all with, a companion, someone like—Unbidden a masculine face, sun-bronzed, with lips that lifted at the corners, invaded her mind. Funny how she couldn't get him out of her thoughts. For the hundredth time during the past few days she thrust the picture aside and endeavoured to concentrate on the present. Tomorrow she would drive around the winding waterfront road that curved close to the sun-sparkled harbour where small bays were clustered with yachts and craft of all description. Or maybe she would take a climb up the mountain that had once been an active volcano, or settle for a ferry trip over the harbour to explore the high volcanic mountain with its ever changing colours. Tomorrow ... lazing on the beach, strolling through green native bush or motoring along surburban streets, the lazy sunsoaked days drifted by. Gradually with them went some of the shock and tension of the past weeks and in its place came a sense of restlessness. Fascinating though she found this colourful city, she had planned to visit other parts of the country, especially the northern areas with their historical landmarks and flawless bays.

'There it is!' Mary's excited tone jerked her from her musing. 'At last, the coast!'

Alison followed her gaze towards the sea of tea-tree at the roadside and beyond to the misty blue of the Tasman. 'Civilisation too!' She was looking up towards a farmhouse set high on the brow of a hill above cleared green slopes. The white-timbered home sprawled against a shelter belt of tall trees.

'Wait! Stop!' Mary jerked her arm so violently that the car swerved to the side, then Alison braked to a sudden stop. 'What on earth——?'

'Didn't you see? The name on the gatepost of that house up on the hill? It was Vasanovich! I didn't think I could be so lucky! I've just got to go up there and find out if it really is that family name of mine. Do you mind?'

'Mind?' Alison turned towards her with a smile. 'I'll come with you.'

CHAPTER THREE

'IT's worth enquiring about anyway,' Mary said as Alison swung into the driveway. 'If it does happen to be one of my long-lost cousins won't Grandfather be pleased!'

'Don't forget,' warned Alison as she slowed to a stop, 'that in the country it's the custom for the passenger to get out and open the gates.'

'It's worth it.' Mary was already opening the car door and running forward. When the Mini was through the opening Mary closed the gate behind them and Alison, putting the vehicle into a low gear, went slowly over the paddock, cutting a trail through the black steers who ambled from approaching wheels at the last moment. They rattled over a cattle stop, then followed the winding track up the grassy slopes. Above, the low ranch-style house lay bathed in afternoon sunshine, orange-tiled roof bright against a backdrop of dark macrocarpa pines. Around the dwelling sloping lawns studded with flowering shrubs fell sharply away to paddocks below. They passed through a second gate, then a third, and soon were skirting a mellow red shearing shed, passing implement sheds, stables and garages.

Alison pulled up at the small gateway leading to the back of the house. 'At least there's someone at home. The door's open and there are children's clothes on the line ... more or less.' She reached up to untangle small garments that were whipped around the line in the prevailing wind. Mary, however, was hurrying ahead up the white-concreted path and knocking on the door leading to a back porch.

There was no answer to the summons and as Alison came to join her Mary knocked again, louder this time. 'If they don't hear that thunderous noise they must be deaf— or miles away.' Still there was no response.

'They must all be outside.' Mary turned away. 'Let's take a look around, shall we?'

Together they climbed a grassy slope behind the house, scanning the vast sheep-threaded hills rising around them. The intense stillness of the country was broken only by the lowing of cattle. Or was there another sound, Alison wondered, a faint echo borne towards them on the wind?

'No luck,' Mary was saying. 'They must have taken off over the hills somewhere.'

'Listen!' Once again Alison caught the faint sound, almost like someone calling for help. There it was again, a feminine voice, calling for help. 'Do you hear what I hear?'

Mary nodded. 'Someone's in trouble. It's coming from just over the hill, but I can't see anyone.'

'Come on!' Alison was hurrying down the slope and Mary ran along beside her. It wasn't until they reached another rise that they caught sight of a tousled grey head apparently protruding from the grassy hillside. There was no doubt about the voice now. 'Help, somebody! Help!'

Alison was the first to reach the middle-aged woman whose grey locks were visible from the opening in the ground in which she was apparently trapped. A farm motorbike lay upturned at her side and the face looking up at them was scarlet with frustration and anger. 'Thank heaven you've come! I've been here for hours, seems like hours anyway! Get me out, will you?'

Obligingly Alison knelt down, extending her hand, but the tall heavy woman released her grip almost immediately, the colour draining away from sun-weathered cheeks.

'You're hurt?' Alison asked gently.

'It's my knee, curse that motorbike! I've put my knee out and it won't take my weight. Even without that, though, I couldn't get out, I'm stuck in this darned hole. I don't suppose either of you can drive a tractor?'

'I can!' With a call to Mary, 'Stay with her till I get back!' Alison hurried away towards the shed. 'I won't be long.'

Presently she came bumping over the grass in the tractor

and soon she was backing the vehicle towards the trapped figure. 'I'm going to winch you out,' she told her. 'Do you think you can hold on to the rope while I winch you up to the tractor?'

'I'll do it,' vowed the angry voice, 'I'll do it if it's the last thing I ever do!'

'Here we go, then! Catch!' Alison tossed the rope down the hole and very slowly winched the woman upwards. Grimly the stranger clung to the rope, her face a deep crimson now with exertion.

'You're going to make it,' encouraged Mary, and at last the woman was free. Mary helped her into the tray of the tractor and steadied her as the tray lifted and they went slowly over the humps and hollows of the grassy paddock. Both girls assisted the stranger up the path and into the house, then with a sigh of relief the woman collapsed into an easy chair in the dining room. 'What a relief!'

'Is your knee very painful?' Mary asked.

'It's not too bad,' but she had tightened her lips. 'I can stand it.'

Mary said, 'What about pain-killer tablets? Have you any in the house?'

'In the bathroom cabinet——'

'I'll get them.' In a flash Mary had left the room.

'As things turned out I'm jolly glad you two girls happened along today.' Alison met the big woman's rakish grin. She was tall and raw-boned, Alison saw now, with a weather-roughened tanned skin, a beaky nose and bright brown eyes. Aloud Alison said, 'If you'll tell me where you keep the brandy——'

Again the rakish grin. 'I'd rather have a cuppa!'

'And so you shall.' Already Alison was plugging in the cord of the electric jug and reaching to a shelf above her head for the pottery teapot. Funny how in farm homes the teapot was invariably kept on a shelf above the sink-bench, together with the tea-caddy.

When the injured woman had swallowed the tablets Mary brought her, and had drunk the hot tea, a little colour returned to the weather-roughened, deeply tanned face. 'You'll feel better after that,' Alison comforted her. 'We'll help you into your room and you can rest up for a while while we ring the doctor. Have you his telephone number handy?'

'It's okay, love, I don't need a doctor. This is something that's happened before, worse luck. It's a weak knee—I hurt it in a fall from a horse last year and it goes out of action at the drop of a hat. It's the remedy I'm worried about. No need to ring the doctor, because I know exactly what he'd say—complete rest for at least two weeks. That's where I'm really in trouble. Thing is,' she went on in a worried tone, 'this darned ulcerated leg of mine,' she indicated the elastic bandage wound tightly around her plump leg. 'The doctor's ordered me to put my foot up, it's the only way, he says, it will ever heal. Now I've opened it up again and with this other trouble on top of it ... I just can't do it!' She put down her teacup with a clatter.

'But you said yourself,' Alison pointed out, 'that nothing else will heal the ulcer——'

'I know, I know, but it's not so easy.'

'It never is in the country,' Alison agreed gently, 'don't I know it!'

'It's a lot worse than you know. This couldn't have happened at a worse time! That darned motorbike—I always said horses were a lot better than bikes on any farm. I never dreamed there was a hole in the ground. The grass had grown over it and the first I knew was finding myself down there with a sharp pain in my knee. That's the trouble when you've taken over a new place, you don't know the ground. If it had been my old home I knew every inch of the land. Now I just don't know what to do.' She seemed thankful to unburden the frantic worry that possessed her. 'They're depending on me, my son and the children——'

'But surely his wife——' Alison murmured.

'No, no, you don't understand. He's not married. The twins are my niece's children. She's my favourite niece too and if I'm stuck in bed for weeks and weeks who's going to look after the family?'

Mary said in a puzzled tone, 'Couldn't the children's mother come and get them? If they're just here on holiday, the twins——'

'No, she and her husband are not even in the country.' Again the note of desperation in her tones. 'I may as well tell you that Karen and her husband,' she drew a shaky breath, 'haven't been getting along well lately. Their marriage is in a pretty precarious state one way and another. All this talk of marriage. counsellors ... I was really worried about them. Then out of the blue came an offer from Switzerland, a chance for them to stay overseas for two months. Ben's a ski-ing instructor, you see, and the experience would mean a lot to him. It was just too good an opportunity to miss, what with the fares paid for both Ben and Karen. The only catch was it would entail a lot of travelling, so of course I offered to look after the twins. I was only too glad to have them, the darlings, and then——' her voice dropped to an exasperated frustrated note, 'this had to happen!'

Sensitive always to another's pain and problems, Alison cried impulsively, 'But that's no problem! I could stay and look after things here until you get on your feet again! My friend Mary and I, we're just touring around the countryside having a look around. I wouldn't mind a bit.'

'Would you really? It just seems too good to be true, your dropping in like this just at the right time.' The eager light in the brown eyes was dashed. 'But what about your own plans?'

'I haven't any!' Alison said cheerfully. 'Nothing that can't be postponed for a few weeks, anyway.'

'I can't believe it! You really will? You won't change your mind?'

'I never go back on a promise,' said Alison gaily.

With the nagging worry removed from her mind the patient brightened. 'Couldn't you stay here too?' She glanced towards Mary. 'There's swags of room and you two could be company for each other. *Please?*'

'I don't see why not.' Mary had a way of talking with her hands, Alison noticed. White hands that unlike her own tanned paws looked as though they had never engaged in any hard physical toil. 'So long as you let me help with things. Who knows?' she smiled her slow sweet smile, 'it might just happen to work in with my own plans.'

'Don't worry,' the older woman appeared delighted with Mary's decision, 'there's plenty to do here both inside and outside the place. I won't mind taking it easy for a while now, not now you two girls are being so good to me, spoiling me and taking over all the chores, and the twins. They're good kids, though, Sue and Patrick, they won't cause you too much worry.'

'We could start,' Mary suggested, 'by making you a bit more comfortable. How about letting us take you to your room and pop you into bed? Then I can bring along a bowl of warm water and clean up some of those cuts and bruises.'

The older woman gazed down at her bare arms, covered with scratches, at the trickle of blood running down below the elastic bandage on her leg. 'I must look a mess.'

'You'll look as good as new once I've done with you,' Mary promised laughingly. The big woman laid an arm around the shoulder of each girl and they proceeded up the long hall and into an end bedroom. While Alison helped her to undress Mary searched in a bureau for a nightdress and before long the patient, freshly washed and cool and comfortable, was settled in her bed.

'Now let me get this right,' she glanced towards Alison, 'you're——?'

'I'm Alison.'

'And your friend is Mary. I'm Frances, by the way. I was so unlucky today falling into that hole—well, not exactly a hole. It's an ancient tunnel the Maoris must have made years and years ago to bring the water from the fresh water lake up to their *pa* at the top of the hill.'

Alison looked surprised. 'How did you know?'

'Oh, I've studied Maori customs quite a lot. As soon as I

42

came across that hill I knew it was the site of an old Maori *pa*. It had all the signs of occupation even if it was a hundred years ago—cooking pits with the grass growing over them, banks of pipi shells. I was so excited about my find then bang, that farm bike tipped me off on a mound of earth and down I went into that hidden tunnel with the grass growing over it.'

For something to say Alison murmured, 'You're interested in Maori archaeology?'

'Oh, more than interested! I'm really keen about finding out all I can about how the Maoris lived before the pakehas arrived here. I've taken a course in Maori language and now I'm doing my best to find out the old Maori proverbs. My aim is to make them into a book when I've discovered enough. Such a pity the race had no written language, just legends and tribal lore passed down by word of mouth or chants or dances. Still, I'm getting quite a few proverbs. Fascinating it is too. They're such a poetical race, the Maoris, with a gift for words, lyrical really, and they can pack a punch when it comes to making up proverbs. You wouldn't believe it,' the excited tones ran on, 'but from what I've been able to find out they had a proverb for almost every possibility.'

Mary tucked an extra pillow beneath the grey hair and taking a hairbrush from the top of the dressing table, ran the brush down the short wiry strands. 'How about your troubles today? Did they have one to cover anything like that?'

'Don't stop brushing, love. It's so soothing to have someone attending to your hair. Oh yes, there's one for what happened to me just awhile ago. I'm putting it in my book under the heading "difficulties overcome". "*He manga wai koia kia kore a whitikia*"—"It's a big river indeed that cannot be crossed." ' All at once her voice was dreamy. 'I can relax now. The twins will be home soon, and my son won't be long after them. He's gone to a stock sale at Dargaville. You'll tell the children, Patrick and Sue, about me? They'll be so upset if they don't see me about when they get back from school.' Fear sharpened her tone. 'You will be here, won't you?' She gazed anxiously from one girl to the other.

'Don't worry, Mrs Vasanovich,' Mary murmured, laying down the hairbrush, for the older woman's eyes were closed and she appeared to be on the verge of sleep. 'We'll take care of everything for you.'

There was no answer and it was clear that the pain-killing tablets were fulfilling their purpose. Presently, when the even breathing assured her the patient was asleep, Alison crept from the room. In the hall Mary was coming towards her, a travel bag in one hand and the cardboard carton in the other. She grinned, her sleepy eyes crinkling with amusement, 'Seeing we're going to move in I thought I'd better get started. I travel light myself—what on earth's in this monstrous carton?'

'Only my saddle.'

'Your *saddle*? Well, one thing, you'll be able to make yourself useful around the place. But of course, you're a country girl, you told me yourself. I was forgetting.'

'Do you think we should call the doctor? Evidently this trouble is something that's happened before, so he'll know how to treat her.'

'Let's leave it until the son comes home, shall we?'

'It might be an idea.' They were moving along the passage together, peering into a bedroom with two single beds covered in cotton spreads, a painted chest of drawers and empty wardrobe.

'This one looks like a guest room.' Mary tossed the luggage on one of the beds. 'We'll share?'

'Yes, of course.' Alison's lips twitched at the corners.

'What's so funny?'

'Oh, nothing really. It was just that something struck me. That Maori proverb Mrs Vasanovich quoted, something about "It's a big river indeed that cannot be crossed." I keep thinking about the big river we crossed today. Seems funny somehow.'

Mary was taking toilet accessories from her canvas pack. 'Not so funny as it's going to be soon when the son comes

44

home and finds two strange girls all nicely settled in his home!'

'You'll have to look after him,' Alison teased. 'He's your second cousin, or something. Me, I'll settle for the twins.'

As if in answer to her words at that moment the murmur of childish voices floated past the open window. Presently there were sounds of the kitchen door being flung open, followed by loud calls of 'Gran! Where are you—can we have a cookie?'

'I'd better go and put them in the picture before they wake her!' Alison hurried on ahead into the kitchen where the five-year-old twins were seated on the floor, busily snapping open the catches of their incandescent pink lunch cases and strewing papers all over the floor.

Cropped dark heads jerked upward as Alison came into the room and two pairs of blue eyes glanced curiously towards her.

'Hi!' She dropped down beside them. 'You're Sue, aren't you, and you're Patrick? I'm Alison and this is my friend Mary. What have you got there?'

'Look, I drew this picture.' Sue was thrusting a crayoned sketch towards her. 'I got a star today.'

'Look at mine,' cried Patrick, 'look at mine first!' He got to his feet, clutching his drawing paper to a small chest. 'Where's Gran? I want to show her my picture.'

'You can't,' Alison told him. 'She's in bed. You mustn't worry her, because she's sick. She's hurt her leg in a fall from her motorbike out in the paddocks. We found her there and brought her inside. Now she has to stay quiet and rest until she's better.'

Anxious-eyed, the children stared up at her. Then with a total lack of sympathy, they wailed in unison, 'But who's going to look after us?'

'We are,' said Mary promptly, 'and that means you'll both have to do as you're told. For a start how about picking up all that mess from the floor and coming to sit at the table while I get you some cool drinks?' She muttered in an aside to Alison, 'I only hope there is something in that line.' She moved towards the large refrigerator in a corner of the room and soon she was pouring chilled orange drinks into plastic beakers and reaching up to a shelf to take down a tin of home-made cookies.

Slightly subdued by two strangers, the twins picked up their sketches and laid them on the table beside them. Gravely Alison inspected the crayoned pictures. 'Very good.' She was gazing down at a coloured sketch of an elongated skinny figure with flyaway hair, bared teeth and staring purple eyes. 'Who's this?'

'Can't you see?' Sue's note was one of exasperation. 'It's Uncle Craig, of course.'

'Is it now?' In the babel of childish voices Alison hadn't heard anyone approach. Now at the deep and amused masculine tone she swung around.

'Uncle Craig!' The children ran to him, both talking at once, as they endeavoured to show him their sketches. Over their heads Alison's distraught gaze met that of the man standing in the doorway. She was unaware that her lips were parted in horrified amazement. It couldn't be, things like this didn't really happen, there must be some ghastly mistake. But deep down where it counted she knew there was no mistaking the man who was entering the room. She would recognise his step anywhere. Here was Craig Carter himself, as coolly confident and—admit it—as disturbingly attractive as ever. The frantic thoughts went whirling through her mind. Then she did a double take. Don't panic. Remember *he doesn't know you. He's never set eyes on you before*. All you have to do is to remember to play your part and he'll never suspect a thing. He mustn't! For the implications of his finding out her true identity just didn't bear thinking about.

'That's enough for now kids. Quiet!' he thundered, and immediately the children's voices subsided.

'I'd better explain.' Alison tried to gather her senses together. If only he wouldn't look at her! There was something in his glance that scattered her thoughts and put everything out of her mind, everything sensible, that is.

46

She took a deep breath. 'My friend—Mary—and I, we happened to come up to the house——' Heavens, but she was making a complete mess of all this, the explanation was becoming so involved——

'That's right,' Mary's quiet voice cut in. Thank heaven the other girl had taken up the narrative. It was different for Mary when it came to explaining their presence here. There were no hang-ups for her concerning one Craig Carter. Alison wrenched her thoughts back to Mary's voice. 'I was hoping to look up some distant relatives of mine and when we noticed the name on the gate I couldn't resist coming up to the house to enquire. You see, my name happens to be Vasanovich too.'

'Now I get it!' His puzzled expression changed to one of enlightenment. 'Sorry to have to tell you, but the family have moved away from here. They're still in the district, but they've invested in a big block of land a bit further north. I took over from them a week ago.'

It all ties in, Alison was thinking. He's bought this place. Probably he's put in managers on the other two properties, but he's living right here. He's the boss and I've promised his mother I'll stay here and look after the family until she's well again. *What have I done?*

'That explains a lot,' Mary was saying in her reflective way. 'When we got to the house we couldn't find anyone at home, though it looked as though the occupants weren't far away. So we went looking up in the back paddocks, heard someone calling and found your mother——'

The smile fled from his lean bronzed face. He said tersely, 'Mum? An accident? That damned motorbike she's so crazy about. Is she all right?'

Mary nodded. 'She's not badly hurt. Seems she took a fall from the bike and landed herself in an overgrown old tunnel on the hillside. She hurt her leg a bit——'

'Put her knee out again, I bet! It happens to her every now and again. She'll be hopping mad if she's forced to rest up for weeks. I'll go and have a word with her.'

'She's asleep,' Mary told him. 'We gave her a couple of

47

codeine to ease the pain. We thought we'd wait until you came home to see about calling a doctor.'

'Good thinking. I sure do appreciate——' He broke off as a strong feminine accent reached them from the direction of the bedroom up the hall. 'Craig, is that you?'

'Be back soon.' Turning on his heel, he hurried from the room.

In the silence the small girl said in a hushed tone, 'Poor Gran, will her leg get better?'

Patrick answered her. 'Course it will. But she won't be able to ride her motorbike.' His tone was tinged with wistfulness. 'I wish I could ride her bike. I bet I could ride a farm bike if I tried——'

'You could not so,' his sister argued repressively, ' 'cause Uncle Craig wouldn't let you—now look what you've done!' For in the argument a beaker of orange drink had spilled to the floor and Alison went in search of a cloth to mop up the sticky liquid.

When she had cleaned the floor the children ran out to play. She became aware of Mary's thoughtful look. 'What were you looking at me in that odd way for a while back? Didn't you want to stay here?'

Alison looked away. 'I can't stay.'

'But you were the one who was all for it. You can't back out now. Why have you changed your mind all of a sudden?'

'Just something I've remembered ... something ...' If only she could explain the truth—but clearly that was out of the question. 'But you can——'

'Well, I'm not staying without you,' Mary declared flatly. 'You're the one who knows all about farm work, meals and all that, it's all Greek to me. Besides, you promised. You can't leave that poor woman in the lurch like that——' She broke off as Craig came back to the room.

Alison decided to throw it over to fate. What else could she do?

'She's doing it hard, having to be laid up.' There was a frown on the bronzed face. 'Says she won't have the doctor

48

—guess she knows what he'll say to her when he sees her! I gave him a buzz from the office and he'll be along to check her over as soon as he can fit it in. Says to keep the patient in bed meantime. I've just been hearing about that offer of yours——' From his height he glanced down at Alison and she wondered if he could sense her nervousness. Why did he seek her out instead of Mary? Mary who was so much older and more capable looking than herself, with her mop of coppery curls and small slim figure? 'She's been letting me in on how you two rescued her today, and better still, that you've offered to stay on in the house keeping things running along until she gets well enough to cope.' His glance towards Alison was deep and intent and somehow very difficult to sustain. He perched his long length on the table and and taking the makings from the pocket of his drill shorts, began leisurely to roll himself a cigarette. As she watched him Alison was reminded of the last occasion on which she had observed him doing just that. He ran his lips along the tissue paper. 'You two dropping in here like this at just the right time seems too good to be true.'

It is. But she said the words silently.

He held a light to his cigarette and blew out the flame. At last, Alison thought, his glance had shifted to Mary. 'It's a terrific stroke of luck, your staying on so far as we are concerned—but,' he was eyeing her narrowly, 'how about you? For all I know it might put finish to some schemes of your own for the next few weeks.'

'Not to worry,' Mary assured him smilingly. 'Honestly, it will be quite an experience for me, staying on a New Zealand sheep farm. I've only been in the country a short while.'

From out of nowhere Alison was assailed by a stab of— could it be jealousy? Ridiculous to feel this way, merely because Mary had confided to her those romantic notions about the Kiwi sheep-farmer breed. Craig Carter meant nothing to her ... on the contrary. Indeed, at this moment she wished him far enough.

'It's a deal, then?'

Frantically Alison strove to catch Mary's eye. Her lips mouthed a soundless NO! and she shook her head vehemently, but Mary merely stared back at her in bewilderment. She had a suspicion that Craig had caught her out and intercepted her silent signal, so she didn't dare repeat the effort, not with those oh-so-perceptive blue eyes once again fixed on her downcast face.

'We couldn't do anything else,' Mary assured him laughingly. 'Your mother was so terribly worried, not about herself, but about the household, and especially the twins. We just had to offer to stay, and it wasn't any sacrifice really. Seeing we're both just touring acround the country it seemed a good idea.'

'It's a fantastic idea!'

A good idea! Alison thought desperately. Surely he must have caught on by this time that no matter how happy Mary is about the arrangement, I'm not keen to stay. He must guess by my silence that I'm not feeling the same way at all, not with him right here in the house, *his* house! But what excuse can I give to get out of staying on? I can't get out of it.

She brought her mind back to Craig's deep tones. 'I can tell you this much. Mum would be more than upset if you two hadn't come to her rescue today. It's about all she seems to be thinking of at the moment—apart from keeping the doctor at bay, that is. Those girls, those two nice girls, they'll stay, both of them ... you see, they *promised.*'

Alison felt slightly sick at the thought that she was the one who had done all the promising. How simple the matter had seemed half an hour ago, and how devastating the position in which she now found herself.

'Great! If you two can stick around until Mum gets mobile again that will suit us fine. She'll put you in the picture about the household chores, the time to get the kids ready for the school bus at the corner of the road down there, all that stuff. Meals shouldn't be too much of a problem. I take off for work fairly early in the day and get back for a late breakfast around eight. I take lunch with me and usually get home about dark. But there's no need for the rest of you to wait dinner for me.' Bushy dark eyebrows lifted enquiringly. 'You've sorted out a room for yourselves?'

'Oh yes.' It was Mary who answered. Alison reflected that he must surely regard her as the most uncommunicative girl he had ever come across. It was as well that Mary was taking all this in her stride, considering the chaotic state of her own feelings. To the other girl all this was merely an interlude, an amusing episode to relate to her friends back home in England when she returned.

'Terrific! I'll make it worth your while financially of course. Good of you both to help us out. The usual wages doubled in this case—no problem. It isn't everyone who'd take on an invalid up in the bedroom at the end of the hall as well as five-year-old twins, and all at a moment's notice!'

Not to mention the one man in the world you're trying to avoid? She realised he was regarding her with his intent look. 'You're very quiet, Miss ——' He broke off. 'I didn't get your name?' Even in the tumult of her emotions she found herself thinking that his smile was really something.

She hesitated for a split second. *Careful, Alison*, you don't want to give the game away right at the outset by some stupid blunder. Very clearly she said, 'It's Wynyard,' and could scarcely believe that the name made no particular impact on him.

'Well, Alison Wynyard, what do you think about the arrangement?' Belatedly she realised he was awaiting an answer to his question, *the* question. She found her voice at last and said thickly, 'There's just one thing——'

'Anything you say. Just say the word——'

She told him. She had intended to say something like, 'I hope you understand, but I may have to leave quite soon. I'm expecting word from home and may have to go unexpectedly? Under his mesmeric dancing gaze, however, the words that came from her lips were quite different. 'Where do you keep the potatoes?'

Suddenly he was light-hearted and friendly. 'Come

along and I'll show you around.' He waited while both girls preceded him out of a side door and they entered a spacious porch. As he flung open the door of a side cupboard they caught sight of bags of potatoes, onions, pumpkins, butternuts and the inevitable kumeras with their lumpy shapes and dark crimson skins. 'In here is the storeroom.' He flung open yet another door and they were looking into a room containing a huge upright freezer and high cupboards stacked with an endless variety of tinned foods. Mary gazed down at the variety of packaged and labelled meats stacked in the long white cabinet. 'What a monstrous deep freeze!'

'Not too big for the Vasanovichs, with four grown sons in the family, all living at home.'

Mary's lips were twitching at the corners. 'No! Not *four* of them, all bachelors?'

'That's right.' He grinned. 'Interesting, isn't it? I'll take you along to meet them one day soon, then it will be over to you.'

'Kissing cousins?'

'Something like that. It's up to you. They tell me,' he added meaningfully, 'that the district here is a bit short on girl-power.'

'Is that why you came?'

Watching the other two laughing together, Alison was once again pierced by that curious pang. Only it couldn't be jealousy, for how could your feelings be stirred by a man you scarcely knew and didn't like anyway?

When they had inspected the pantry with its long shelves of packaged foods and jars of home preserves ('Mum brought those jars of apricots up from the South Island,' he told them) they went up the passage and into the bedroom where Frances lay on the bed, her cheeks slightly flushed, her eyes excited.

'Well, old lady, how are you feeling now?'

Frances apparently saw nothing untoward in her son's form of endearment. She grinned cheerfully. 'Never mind about me! I was right, wasn't I?' she queried triumphantly. 'The girls are staying, both of them?'

'That's right,' he assured her. 'We've got it all jacked up. Not that you deserve treatment like that, careering along on that farm bike over hills when you're supposed to be taking care of your ulcerated leg. You don't need to take a course in Maori, what you should be studying is survival training! I told you to watch it——'

Frances looked unrepentant. 'I might have known!' She appealed to the girls standing near the bed. 'You see how it is—no feeling from him, no sympathy.' But the brown eyes softened as they rested on the tall man gazing down at her. 'I just don't know what I would have done without your kind offer, girls.'

The answer came promptly in deep masculine tones. 'You'd have got Karen and Ben back from their cruise ship and sent the kids packing, that's what!'

'Oh, I couldn't do that, Craig!'

'Why not?'

'You know why I couldn't bring your cousin and her husband back right at the start of their holiday. It would spoil everything. One of my Maori proverbs puts it beautifully.'

'I knew it!' groaned Craig. 'The Maoris had one to cover every eventuality and a few more besides, according to Mum! Okay,' he grinned goodhumouredly, 'we're listening, old lady. You've got yourself a captive audience. Fire ahead!'

Taking no notice of his raillery, Frances reached towards a bulky folder lying on the bedside table. 'It's one about marriage,' she murmured, riffling through the loose handwritten pages. 'Got it!' she announced triumphantly, and slowly voiced the soft Maori syllables. ' "*He hono tangata e kore e motu kapa te taura waka e motu.*" '

'Don't look at me,' laughed Mary, glancing up into Craig's dark face, 'I'm fresh out from London.'

At Alison he didn't look, and all at once piqued, she heard her own voice saying quickly, 'A human bond cannot be severed unlike the mooring rope of a canoe which can easily be broken.'

In the startled silence she was aware of Craig's dark-blue eyes, a flicker of amusement in their depths.

'Oh, it was easy for me to pick up some of the Maori language. I was brought up in——' a warning red light flashed in her mind and she broke off, to go on in some confusion, 'in the depths of the country. At the school a lot of the children were Maori, families of the timber workers in the bush. I couldn't help picking up some of the Maori words and a few of their sayings too.'

'Did you hear that?' Craig grinned down at his mother. 'Man, are you on to a good thing I'd say this was your lucky day, accident and all!'

A little later as the two girls were preparing the evening meal, Alison paused in her task of slicing bread, her eyes thoughtful. She had told no one of her change of name, it had all come about so suddenly—and anyway, it was her secret. The fewer people in whom she confided the less chance of Craig Carter discovering her identity, just supposing he did have any ideas in the matter of easing his conscience in that direction. Probably she was worrying needlessly, but supposing he put the matter in the hands of a private enquiry agent? The thought made her say diffidently to Mary, 'If you don't mind there's something I'd like to ask you—a favour. Look, don't say anything to anyone here about the accident—my parents, you know?'

'Oh, I won't! I do understand how you feel. Having folks talk about it must bring it all back. You can depend on me to keep quiet.'

With a lighter heart Alison knew that she could trust her new friend to keep her word.

A few minutes later the doctor arrived at the house. A small man with a lined face and tired smile, he said to the girls, 'Dr Anderson's my name. My patient will be up the hall, I expect,' and went striding up the passage.

From somewhere in the paddocks behind the house Craig must have caught sight of the unfamiliar car in the drive, for shortly afterwards he came strolling into the room just as the doctor returned. Craig introduced himself and the two men shook hands.

'What's the verdict, doctor?'

'Just as I thought. The knee's out of action for a week or two, an old injury it seems. The ulcer will take time to heal. Your mother's put up a good fight, but I managed to convince her that a month's complete rest for her is a must, feet up and no running around after the kids. She had no excuse for not obeying orders after she'd let on about the minor miracle that happened along here today with two helpers strolling along to rescue her and offering to stay on to give her a hand with the chores for a few weeks. Wish my wife could be as lucky. Domestic helpers these days are like gold-dust.' He smiled his jaded smile. 'Even unattractive ones! Well, that's about it. Keep her quiet and make her rest.' He was writing on a pad. 'I'll prescribe something to hurry up the healing and you can pick it up tomorrow in town. I'll call back in a couple of weeks to check up on her progress. Meanwhile,' his glance included both girls, 'I know I'm leaving her in good hands.'

When Alison took the tastefully arranged tea-tray into the bedroom Frances was sitting up in bed, a cheerful grin lighting her lined face.

'I hear,' Alison put down the tray on the bed, 'that the doctor argued you into staying put for a few weeks.'

Frances chuckled. 'Hadn't a leg to stand on! Oh well, I don't mind so much now. One thing, I've got plenty to keep me occupied.' She sent a distasteful glance towards the knitting wool, needle and pattern on the low table beside her. 'Plenty I *should* be doing, I should say.'

'You like knitting?'

'Hate it,' Frances answered cheerfully. 'It's so slow, and the wretched things never turn out anything like they look in the books. I know I should be knitting for the twins,' her face brightened, 'but it's such a marvellous chance to get on with my book. I'm putting all the proverbs together, or trying to. After all, it's time someone collected them all. That's one reason I was so glad when Craig decided to take over this place. There are so many Maori people in the North and I might find a few new proverbs, though I've already got swags of them. Now I'm working on the translations, and that's where I'll be calling on you for help. Sometimes there just doesn't seem the right word in our language to match the meaning.' Launched on her hobby, Frances' character-lined face was alive with interest. 'Would you believe that I haven't been able to come across any Maori word meaning "the day after tomorrow" or "day before yesterday"?'

'There isn't one, as far as I know. I guess it was because they thought those times didn't really matter ... only today. Maybe they had something there. May I see your list?'

'I'll show them all to you tomorrow. I'm keeping you from your meal, child. Now you go right back to the others.'

Alison, who was feeling decidedly uneasy at the prospect of sitting down at table to this first meal with *him*, made a further effort at postponing her arrival back in the kitchen. She dropped down on the bed. 'I don't mind.'

But Frances, who in some respects appeared to be as forceful as her son, waved the offer away. 'Now you're not to worry about me, I'm quite all right. The pain's a lot better now and I'm going to enjoy this meal I haven't prepared myself—children behaving themselves?'

'Oh yes. Mary's got them bathed and in their pyjamas ready for bed.'

'Good for her! Now I can really relax. Now off you go, love!'

At the table she found the others waiting for her. The children were chattering and Mary was trying in vain to restore order. Craig's quiet, 'That's enough now, kids!' brought a silence that lasted for exactly two minutes, then broke out the childish voices again. 'I found a kingfisher's nest in the bank today!'

'Yea, and there were babies in it. You could hear them, squeak! squeak! squeak!'

'Another squeak out of either of you two,' Craig thundered, 'and you'll have tea on your own!'

56

This time silence prevailed, a silence that Alison found disconcerting. She was thankful when Mary queried Craig about farming methods in the north and before long he was drawing her out as to her life in England and her recent air trip out to New Zealand. Inevitably the subject of travel led to the Vasanovich family. Alison found herself hoping that with a bit of luck the Vasanovichs would last them until the end of the meal. Anything was preferable to answering questions concerning who she was and where she came from, questions for which she had no answers. She must take no chances of Craig Carter putting two and two together and coming up with the truth.

That evening she sat up in bed in her green shortie-pyjamas of sprigged cotton. Her hands were clasped around tanned knees and tendrils of hair still damp from the shower curled around her forehead. 'He's autocratic and domineering,' she was scarcely aware that the dreamy tones were voicing her thoughts, 'just like I thought he would be.'

Mary spun around from the bureau mirror, a hairbrush suspended in her hand and long black hair streaming over her shoulders. 'You thought? How could you know anything about him?'

'Oh, I don't! I don't!' Swiftly Alison gathered her wits together. 'It was just something his mother said,' she added hurriedly.

'Did she? I didn't notice.' Mary pulled her hair over one shoulder and resumed her brushing. 'I thought he was rather nice ... terribly attractive.'

'Yes, you would, the Kiwi sheep farmer image.' Alison couldn't understand why she was feeling so suddenly out of sorts, as though her skin didn't quite fit and everyone hated her. Aiming a punch at the pillow, she flung herself down and turning her face to the wall made a pretence of going to sleep.

CHAPTER FOUR

WHEN Alison awoke the next morning a glance towards the other bed told her Mary was still asleep. She dressed quickly and went into the opposite room where she could hear the twins chattering together. 'Hello, you two! How about getting yourselves dressed?' She was sorting small clean garments from a drawer in the bureau and laying them on the bed. Then with a final reminder to wash their faces and to brush their hair she went into the kitchen.

Craig would have left the house and started his work hours earlier, probably at daybreak. She could relax for a while free of his disturbing presence. She set the table, found cornflakes, butter, milk and marmalade, and soon the twins were eating breakfast. The children's endless chatter left her free to pursue her own troubled thoughts, for how ever she was going to get through a month of living here in enemy territory, *knowing what she did* . . .

Patrick's excited voice broke into her musing. 'Can I wake Mary up?'

'Let me! Let me!' clamoured his sister.

'Okay. You can both go in when you've finished your breakfast.'

A few minutes later, a piercing scream came from the direction of Mary's bedroom. 'What on earth——?' Alison hurried away to find a terrified Mary standing at the foot of the bed. Of the twins there was no sign.

'What is it? What is it?' Mary cried. 'I'm terrified of insects, I always have been!' She shuddered. 'Ugh, isn't it horrible—is it poisonous, do you think? I might have died——' She was gazing in horror at the big dark insect with its long feelers moving over the pillow.

'It's only a weta——'

'Only! It could kill you, I know it could! It looks evil!

Those little monsters, they crept in here, then they let that thing out of a box and put it down on the pillow! They said you told them to wake me up.'

'It does look horrible,' Alison admitted. 'It could give you quite a nip with those long feelers too, but it wouldn't kill you. Get dressed in the kids' room and I'll get Craig to deal with it when he comes in.'

With a last shuddering glance towards the insect Mary snatched up her garments and hurried away. In the confusion Alison heard Frances' forceful tones echoing down the hall. 'Have those kids been up to their tricks on you girls? I heard a scream and saw them both running outside. They're hiding in the shed. Don't stand any nonsense now. Get Craig to deal with them when he comes. He'll soon settle all that!'

'I'll do that,' Alison told Frances as she reached the bedroom. Privately she reflected that Craig was in for a busy morning. When he arrived back, however, a rather subdued pair of twins had already left the house to wait on the main road below for the arrival of the school bus. Alison could hear Craig in the washroom off the porch and a little later he was in the room, facing her with his warm disturbing smile. 'You're on duty, I see. How's the old lady feeling this morning?'

It was easier, she found, if she didn't look directly into his eyes. 'She had a good night.' A smile tugged at her lips. 'She's been waiting for you to get back——'

'That's mother love for you!'

'To administer justice—will two eggs suit you with bacon and tomatoes?'

'Please—Don't tell me, let me guess. It's the twins again, up to their usual tricks. I'll kill that Patrick if he's been putting insects in your bed! Scared the wits out of you, did he?'

'Not me.' Alison turned the sizzling bacon on the stove, switched on the coffee percolator and cut bread for toast all in quick succession. 'It was Mary who got the treatment.'

'They *said* they were waking me up.' Mary stood in the

doorway, relaxed now and smiling, pushing the dark hair back behind her ears. 'Alison said it was a—a weta.' She shuddered in spite of herself. 'It's still there, in the bedroom. I shut the door and left it. Alison said you would know what to do.'

'No problem. I'll just have a word with Mum.'

When he came back to the kitchen Alison had the eggs cooked to a turn and the appetising aroma of percolating coffee stole through the sunshiny room.

'She's not in any pain,' he said with satisfaction, seating himself at the table. 'Sit down and have coffee with me?'

'I've just finished breakfast,' Alison said quickly. 'I was thinking I could take a run into town this morning and pick up the prescription from the chemist.'

'Not to worry. I've got to shoot through today to pick up a tractor part and get some machinery replacements. When you move into a new place there's a heck of a lot of sorting out to be done. Actually I had quite a decision to make over the past few weeks. I'd made up my mind last year to get rid of the station I was running in the South Island and to come north. Then something came up out of the blue—a property that I inherited down country, a good productive place it is too. Good grassland, ample rainfall with none of the summer droughts that make life such a problem up here. Trouble was the place that was left to me wasn't big enough by half for me. I tried to buy land near to it, but there was none offering, so in the end I bought this place and sold the other.'

Alison was very still. 'You—sold it?' Dismay and shock got the better of her and even to her own ears the words were fraught with emotion. She couldn't help it. Banner— what had become of Banner? Had Mr Black kept his word about caring for her white show-jumper? The terrible part of it all was that she couldn't even ask about the mare. Thank heaven he hadn't appeared to notice the untoward emotion in her voice.

'That's right.' He was rolling a cigarette, spilling tobacco along the flimsy paper.

'I mean,' wildly Alison jabbered on in an attempt to cover the slip, 'it seems a pity, if the place down country was in such wonderful order.'

'You reckon?' He looked up at her, eyeing her with his brilliant gaze, but now she had herself well in hand. 'You haven't seen this place yet. It's quite something. High hills, fresh-water lakes to take care of the droughts that seem to be the main disadvantage around the place—know anything about sheep farming, Miss Wynyard?'

'Alison.' She began gathering up plates from the table. 'A bit. I used to live in the country.' For a long moment she feared he was about to enquire the whereabouts of her home, but then she realised with relief that she need not have concerned herself on that score. 'I'll tell you something, this place is worth having. Peringales are a new breed to me, they're different from the Romneys I was running down south. They look different and they don't act like the others.'

'Oh, I know! I know! They're so much more alert and intelligent. Look at them now——' She moved to the window looking across at the high grassy hill close by where sheep flowed over the tracks on the hillside like a white river.

He followed her gaze. 'At first I thought the dogs were moving them, but it seems they're just playing. They do that most mornings about this time. After a while they're puffing like hell, but they don't stop. There they go!' The white mass spread over the hillside, then as if at a given signal, turned and pelted back the way they had come.

'I'll take you out for a look around when I get back from Dargaville.' There was no doubt who gave the orders around here, Alison mused. 'Bring Mary too if she'd like a run out. Mum will be all right on her own for an hour or so.'

At that moment Mary came into the room. 'I've been up with Frances,' she smiled. 'She says she's feeling as comfortable as can be and she can't wait to get on with her notes. She was telling me there's a typewriter in the office,

61

so I'll be able to type the pages out for her when she's got them ready.'

'Help yourself!' Craig gestured towards a small room off the passage. 'Come to that, I could do with some help myself with the paper-work. How lucky can a guy get? Alison here to cope with the domestic chores and a private nurse-cum-secretary as well!'

For no reason at all Alison felt hurt and angry. It was always the same where she was concerned. She remembered the lawyer's dampening advice to her concerning job-seeking. 'Plenty of domestic work available on the farms.' For Mary, the interesting task of keeping his books, helping him compile tax returns, profit-and-loss accounts, stock sheets, important things like that, while for her—she clattered the dishes in the sink.

Over the clink of crockery she caught Craig's lazy tones. 'Care for a look around the place, Mary? I'm taking off soon with Alison on a sight-seeing tour, so——'

Mary picked up a tea-towel. 'Thanks, but could I come another time?' Alison couldn't understand her secret pleasure at the words, especially as she liked Mary. 'Your mother might just need something and I'd rather be handy.'

'Good of you.'

'It's not really.' She smiled her slow sweet smile. 'I was telling Alison I've always been sorry I didn't take up nursing, I got shuffled off into office work at the beginning and afterwards it seemed a bit late to change jobs. You're really doing me a favour, if you could call helping Frances to get on with her Maori proverb book nursing! Anyway, there's someone I want to get in touch with, and I thought I'd give them a ring. You did say the Vasanovichs still live in the district?'

'Sure they do. I got it from Papa Vasanovich himself— the address. The phone number's on the pad by the telephone. Two of the sons were running sheep and steers on land a bit further away, then they decided they'd team up with the parents and get a family farm. So if you ring through to that number you'll be in touch with the family all in one go. Did you tell me you were a relation?'

Mary laughed. 'A distant connection, more like it. The name's the same, so that's a start. I've got a grandfather back in England who's very anxious for me to look up any of the family I can find. Rumour has it they settled here in the old gum-digging days, so ... It's all pretty vague really, but I'll get in touch with this family now that I'm here.'

'Why not?'

Craig left the house shortly afterwards. Alison could see his dust-spattered car moving down the main road. To her, sweeping and vacuuming, washing out children's garments, whipping up a batch of fluffy scones for morning cuppa, it seemed no time at all until he was back. Strong and vital, he seemed to bring a breath of the outdoors with him, or was it some masculine magnetism, Alison wondered, that made her so acutely *aware* of him? She could catch his deep tones as he spoke with his mother, then he came back to the kitchen where she had cups laid out on the table.

'Hmm, smells good.' He had lifted the cloth covering a plate of warm scones.

'I'll just take some tea up to your mother.'

'Thanks, love.' Frances made room for the tray amidst the handwritten pages that entirely covered the bed. 'Now you go right back with the others. I'll be fine.'

Alison found Craig explaining to Mary various aspects of sheep farming in New Zealand. 'You'll see what I mean when you get around the paddocks. Ever been on the back of a tractor? Or out in a Land Rover? Some spots up here in the hills are pretty inaccessible.'

Mary shook her head.

'There's always a first time.'

'But not just now,' Mary protested. 'I'm waiting for a call back from the Vasanovichs. I rang through and some-one, it must have been the father, said he'd get his wife to ring me the moment she came in from outside. She was feeding the calves or something.'

'Sounds like a farmer's wife. I got the idea when I met

the family that Papa Vasanovich leaves all the big decisions to Mama.' Craig swung around to face Alison. 'How about you? Feel like coming out with me for a look around the place?'

There was no escape, no real reason why she shouldn't go with him. It was an ordinary enough request, she knew. Being alone with the boss was just one of the problems she must cope with here. She would be fine so long as she kept a constant watch on her impulsive tongue and didn't spoil everything with some stupid remark. She nodded carelessly. 'If you like. I'll just fix the dishes.'

'You won't, you know,' Mary told her, 'you'll leave them to me. Off you go, and have fun!'

Fun! Reluctantly Alison rose from the table and accompanied Craig out into the sunshine. Yet seated beside him on the high seat of the Land Rover, unexpectedly she was swept by a surge of wild sweet happiness. It must be something to do with the warmth and sunshine, the translucent blue sky against which the pine plantations were cut so sharp and clear.

They swept past the implement sheds and garages and took a track up a rise, two sheepdogs running alongside. All at once Craig braked to a stop and Alison wondered why. Then she realised the reason, for there in a grassy paddock sheltered by tall leafy trees she saw her own graceful white mare. He was out of the vehicle and strolling towards the paddock, but Alison was quicker still, hurrying ahead and flinging open the gate. In that moment she forgot everything but Banner, who was nickering softly as she came trotting towards her. The mare reached her and Alison, gently stroking the white muzzle, was scarcely aware of the masculine tones. 'She's not mine. Actually she belongs to a girl down country on the other property. I'm just taking care of the mare until the owner comes to collect her.'

'Oh.' Alison bent her head to hide her scarlet cheeks and went on stroking the white muzzle. For something to say she murmured in a muffled tone, 'When?'

He shrugged. 'Your guess is as good as mine. She's going

to get in touch when she's found a place of her own, some-where to keep the mare. Mean while,' his gaze was disturb-ing and difficult to sustain, especially with those pink cheeks, 'why don't you try her out?'

'Me?' Now she had no need to feign astonishment. 'How do you know I can ride?'

He laughed. 'Anyone ever told you you've got a very ex-pressive face? The way you were drooling over that mare when I caught up with you just now . . . you can't tell me you're not a horse-lover.'

She nodded, feeling her way carefully. 'I've always loved horses. I can ride—a little.' No need to let on about being a show-jumper. The thoughts chased one another through her mind. How difficult it was to dissemble and pretend . . . and how hard to make herself remember.

'Well then, here's a job for you if you'll take it on. How about your keeping the mare in trim? Feeding, exercising, grooming—you know what to do. Interested?'

'Oh, that would be fabulous!' Pure happiness made her forget to be careful. She reached out a hand and affection-ately patted the mare's thick white chest. 'You'd like that, wouldn't you, Banner?'

She realised her blunder the moment the words were out.

He was quick to pick her up. 'How come you know her name?'

She turned her face aside to hide her confusion. She seemed to be always turning her face away this morning. 'Just a guess,' she mumbled, 'a lucky guess.' The words came quickly, jerkily. 'I mean, at shows——' another blun-der. She prayed he wouldn't notice the slip—'you often come across white horses called Banner . . . or Blue . . . or Misty.' She heard herself babbling wildly on. 'Haven't you noticed?'

'I've noticed.'

She didn't quite trust the thoughtful glance he was send-ing her. Could he possibly suspect the truth? But no, that was ridiculous. It was only her own guilt that prompted her to read a special significance in his tone.

'Why don't you try her out?' he suggested once again.

'I will ... sometime.' His look was hard to meet.

Back in the Land Rover they lurched and bumped over the grassy paddocks with the dogs leaping alongside the wheels and sheep scattering in panic at their approach. They swept past a mellow red timber building that was the shearing shed, climbed up a steep slope. Now the wind was stronger, tearing at Alison's hair, sending the short curls blowing around her face. Around them drifted an elusive perfume, sweet as frangipani, but how could that be, she wondered, away up here miles from anywhere?

He seemed to read her thoughts. 'Can't you guess what it is? The cabbage tree perfume drifts for miles on the wind.'

She gazed towards the clumps of palm-like trees dotting the slopes around them. High at the top amidst the tangled green banners fluttering in the wind, she caught sight of a shower of creamy-pink blossoms.

They were sweeping up a steep grassy hillside and soon he was bringing the Land Rover to a stop just below the summit. As they got out to climb the last few feet of the rise Craig took her hand in his and once again for no reason at all Alison felt ridiculously happy, evasions and all.

They stood on the narrow point in the shadow of a concrete reservoir, evidently erected on the highest point of land. The wind was stronger than ever here, whipping Alison's jeans around her legs and fluttering her cotton blouse against her slim figure. Beyond was the misty blue of the Tasman and near at hand rose high sandhills, the sand endlessly moving in the restless wind.

'They had to plant the marram grass and put in pine plantation to save the land around here,' Craig was saying, and she followed his gaze to the marram grass creeping up the slopes. 'Survival tactics, otherwise the drifts of sand would have covered the lakes in the prevailing wind, and the paddocks too, just as they have over there——' Gently he put a hand to her tanned cheek, turning her head away, and for a dizzy moment Alison's emotions soared, quivering like the shimmering sun on the sandhills. The next moment she recovered herself, becoming aware of the tops of tall tea-tree protruding through the sand.

'Goodness, it must have taken quite a time for the trees to be covered like that,' she murmured breathlessly.

'Not so long as you'd think. Without the pines and the marram grass the whole of the property would be lost over a period of years—come on, I'll show you Swan Lake, just over the next rise.'

Once again he took her hand. Was it his touch or her own clumsiness that made her stumble on the dry broken ground as she jumped down? Luckily he arrested her fall and before she could tumble headlong down the slope he had caught her in strong arms, arms that held her a minute longer than need be, a minute while she could feel the beating of his heart through the thin cotton of his shirt. He released her with a quizzical glance that told her that he too had been conscious of the brief physical contact. He said nothing, however, and the next moment he was holding open the heavy door of the vehicle against the prevailing wind.

On and on, climbing slopes so steep that nearing the summit they could see nothing beyond a green peak and a patch of blue sky. Then plunging down over winding sheep tracks while the curious black steers eyed them from adjoining hills. At length they lurched up to the summit of yet another rise and Craig braked to a stop. 'There it is, down there—Swan Lake—see what I mean?'

Alison drew in a sharp breath of wonder. 'I would never have believed it! It's exactly the shape of a swan, even to the long curve of the neck and spread wings.' For far below glimmered a lake in a giant swan shape, the rippled blue waters surrounded by densely growing tea-tree with its filmy mist of white blossom.

'I got a shock when I saw it first too, and that was only last week. When Papa Vasanovich told me about it I took it he meant a lake with swans on it, and that was right too.'

'I see what you mean.' Alison's fascinated gaze was fixed on blue waters, ruffled by the wind, where black swans sailed close to the banks or sought for food amongst raupo and flax growing at the lake edge. As they plunged on down the slope she said with a smile, 'Mary should have come with us. She'd have liked all this. It would have been an experience for her.' Even as she spoke, however, a traitorous thought intruded. She was glad Mary hadn't come with them today, and that was odd, because she liked Mary a lot and Craig Carter she didn't like one little bit ... at least ...

She realised they were nearing the foot of the hill and presently Craig was bringing the vehicle to a stop. He pushed a way through tall tea-tree and soon they had reached the water's edge. Already black swans were swimming away from the shore, gliding out into the centre of wind-stirred waters.

'Lovely,' she murmured, as they moved away.

'There's another lake yet,' he told her as they made their way back to the Land Rover, 'one without all the bush around it where we can swim.'

Soon she realised they were ascending yet another rise and in a few minutes they came in sight of a lake, larger than the other two they had seen, where grass grew down to the water's edge. As they strolled towards the water Craig said, 'According to the locals I've talked to, they've had drought after drought up here for the past five summers. Luckily these lakes never run dry.' He turned towards her and she caught the warmth in the dark blue eyes. 'I'll take you swimming here next week. It's a date.'

'Love to.' Her pulses leaped at the thought of swimming in the clear lake water *with him*. She made an effort to curb her emotions which seemed to be getting out of hand. He was altogether too disturbingly attractive. But that was no reason for her to lose her wits over him. She said, trying for lightness, 'It would be a great place to bring the twins for a picnic. They'd like that.'

'We'll do that too some time.' His tone was careless. You simply couldn't win with him.

All at once she realised that the elusive perfume was becoming stronger, wafted towards them in drifts of sweetness. Although she couldn't see them there must surely be cabbage trees growing nearby.

They strolled on over the cleared ground towards a patch of thickly-growing native bush. They were so close to the sandhills now that at the far part of the bush, tall trees were all but covered in drifting sand. Soon they were climbing over a gate and all at once they were in the cool fragrance of leafy undergrowth where the ground was mossy and damp underfoot and the air spiced with the pungent odour of the bush.

'This happens to be a bird sanctuary,' Craig told her as the silvery notes of a tui cascaded in a flood of melody around them, 'and I'm going to see that it stays that way! Even in this remote area there aren't many stands of native bush left. They were burnt out early-on, more's the pity.'

They emerged at last into sunlight near the lake edge. A timber fence ran out into the water. 'Just to keep the stock out,' Craig explained.

But Alison's attention had been caught by a cabbage tree that had fallen across the fence. Above the floating green banners just clear of the lake water she glimpsed the drifts of the gossamer pink and white blossom. No wonder the cabbage tree flowers had perfumed the air for miles around.

She was kicking off her rubber 'jandals', running ahead of him, throwing over her shoulder, 'I'm going to get some of that cabbage-tree flower to take back to the house——'

'Don't be a fool, Alison, come back——'

She only laughed and sped on. Quick as a wink she leaped up on to the narrow timber railing of the fence and poised on the top rail, made her way, one foot over another, towards the fallen tree.

'You'll be sorry,' he warned. 'Those timbers are rotten——' She took no notice. 'I don't care.' But she was mighty careful all the same, picking her way like a tightrope walker along the narrow rail. She would hate to prove him right after all. A warning crack alerted her to danger and a piece of rotting timber fell into the water below, scaring away a black swan swimming nearby.

'It's not worth it!'

She didn't dare turn around.

'It is to me!'

She reached the fallen tree at last and taking care not to overbalance, managed to reach down and pluck an armful of the clustered pink and white blossoms. Now she had only to make her way back along the rail. Another portion of rotting fence broke away as she turned, but she was safely past the danger spot. Only another few feet ... She allowed herself to hurry and then she felt the railing sag beneath her. Another moment and she would have been in the water giving a disgraceful exhibition of herself as a wet rat, but Craig had moved fast. No doubt he had been expecting this to happen all along, for he had splashed through the water towards her and caught her in his arms. He waded towards the bank and up on to the grass. Once again he was in no hurry to release her and Alison was caught in a moment of heady excitement that was somehow all mixed up with the sweetness of the cloud of blossom crushed between them. It seemed an age until she came back to reality and he dropped her lightly to the springy grass below.

'You did warn me,' she said unsteadily. Then, looking down at his dripping shorts and wet legs, 'You're soaked ——!'

He grinned. 'All in the day's work! Last week it was a stray steer that went into the drink and had to be rescued. One thing's for sure, I'll have to repair that fence before I lose any of the stock.'

So—he placed her in the same category as the wayward steer, Alison thought resentfully. The wild excitement of the moment fled, blown like a puff of thistledown in the strong wind from the ocean. And just as well too, she told herself, a man like that. There was something about him, a masculine magnetism there was no denying. This was something she hadn't bargained for. She would have to be on her guard against her own feelings from now on.

Presently they were back in the Land Rover and lurching over the hills once again. Alison didn't know whether she was glad or sorry that they were moving back in the direction of the house.

She brought her mind back to what he was saying. 'You haven't told me much about yourself——'

The red light flashed on in her mind. 'Nothing much to tell.' Quickly she ran on. 'I'm up in this part of the country on holiday, happened to run into Mary in Dargaville and we decided to join forces. She was free-wheeling around too, so——'

'A holiday from what? Office, shop? Somehow you don't strike me as on office girl. Let me guess——'

His sideways glance took in the clear tanned skin innocent of make-up, the bright mass of curly coppery-red curls tossing around her forehead. 'You worked in the country, right?'

'In a way.' He was getting uncannily near the truth.

'Land Girl? Or how about a supervisor of correspondence lessons for kids on a back-country farm?'

'Land girl's near enough,' she said cautiously. There was no need to explain the exact locality of her duties.

'Brought up in the country, I bet?'

He had caught her off guard. 'Does it show so much?'

He flashed her a sideways grin. 'Does it ever! The way you handle meal times up at the house. No need to tell you about a sheep farmer's hours—and other things. So don't think you can put anything over me,' he was making fun of of her of course, nothing more, 'because I'm warning you I'll catch you out every time! Your face is a dead giveaway, for one thing!'

Golly, he was on about her expression again, and how could she do anything about that? It wasn't going to be easy to keep her identity a secret from him that was for sure, yet somehow she had lost all desire to escape. What if he did imagine he could see through her deceptions with ease, even guess at her thoughts from the way she looked, she could outwit him. It was a challenge she was beginning to enjoy.

71

'And you ride to shows and gymkhanas?' His tone was deceptively careless, but now she had her wits about her.

'Oh, that was ages ago, when I was young.'

'Young?' His quizzical gaze swept the sensitive young face with its soft lips and downcast eyes. 'I thought maybe I could rope you in for the local hunt, you and Banner?'

The temptation to agree was overwhelming, almost, but she forced herself to resist, said on a sigh, 'Oh no, I couldn't!'

'I'll change your mind about that one of these days.' He seemed quite confident in the matter.

They swept past the swan-shaped lake in its setting of thickly-growing tea-tree and moved on over the hills. After a time they approached the paddock where Banner was grazing, but alerted to danger, Alison averted her gaze, even though it was an effort to do so.

'You still haven't told me about yourself,' he reminded her as they approached the house.

She sent him a glance of mock-exasperation. 'What was it you wanted to know?'

'Well, you could fill me in on the important bits like——' his tone softened and she found she was holding her breath, 'boy-friends? Any special guy who might be missing you, inclined to follow you up here?'

'Oh, *that*!' She laughed, relieved that the question had not been the one she had dreaded—Where exactly did you live before you turned up here, Alison? What place? Which farm? 'That's the least of my worries!' and thought how true were the words.

He said quietly, 'That's all I wanted to know.' Suddenly he frowned angrily. 'Hell! Look at those steers! They've broken through from the hill paddocks. The Vasanovichs weren't too particular about their fences. I'll have my work cut out for weeks replacing them.'

Alison thought, bless the Vasanovichs and their unreliable ageing fences. At least it had served to change the subject.

72

'This is quite a big place. What other staff have you?'

There was a glint in his eyes as he raised bronzed well-shaped hands. 'Just these.'

Alison laughed in spite of herself.

CHAPTER FIVE

SHE put problems from her mind as they lurched and bumped their way over the rough grassy slopes. He went on to talk of farming matters, of the differences in climate and soil conditions between North and South Islands as affecting sheep-farming, and Alison was content to listen. She didn't really care what he spoke about (so long as it wasn't anything concerning her own affairs) in that rich deep voice that was almost caressing.

When they got back to the house she found two big jars and filled them with puffs of fragile pink and white blossom. The perfume drifted through the house.

Mary had already sliced cold lamb and prepared a green salad for lunch. Alison made a mental note that she and Mary must organise some sort of work programme between them. The thought, however, brought with it a depressing reminder that she was good only for the domestic side of things, or so Craig imagined.

As they sat down to the meal Alison asked Mary, 'Did you come to any arrangement with the Vasanovichs?'

Mary smiled her sleepy-eyed smile. 'I thought you'd never ask! They're coming to collect me this evening and take me to their place. That is,' she threw Craig an enquiring glance, 'if it's okay with you?'

'Good as gold.'

'So far as I can work out, they're not actually related to me, just connections by marriage, but at least it's something, and won't Grandfather be pleased when he hears about it? They're a distance away, about an hour's drive, but they didn't seem to worry about it. They were thrilled to hear from me—nice too.'

'Better watch it,' Craig warned with his teasing grin, 'four bachelors in one family! You could take your pick, you wouldn't even need to change your name!'

Mary laughed. 'That's what Frances has been telling me. I've been helping her to sort out her notes and she found a Maori proverb to suit the occasion. Something about the attraction of women. I wasn't very flattered, actually.'

'What was it?' Alison enquired.

Mary helped herself to salad. 'I can't remember the Maori words, but it all boiled down to "A handsome man will not be sought after, but even a plain woman will be run after eagerly." '

'You never know your luck,' Alison said demurely. 'After all, it's bachelor territory up here.'

Immediately she regretted the words. Who wouldn't, with Craig throwing her that quizzical make-of-it-what-you-like look?

'Frances is determined to come down to the dining room tomorrow,' Mary reported. 'She says she can keep her leg up on a stool. She seems to think she's missing out on things, being stuck up there in the bedroom.'

'That's an idea,' Alison said. 'She could rest up here just as well.'

'And keep her finger on things,' put in Craig. 'It might be an idea at that, save a devil of a lot of hawking trays around all day.'

He's thoughtful too, Alison told herself, then brought her thoughts up with a jerk. Too! What was she thinking? Merely because he chanced to be attractive in a rugged, take-it-or-leave-it sort of way that was no reason for her to keep thinking about him. She took herself firmly in hand. He's not for you. Remember, Craig Carter is the one man in the world with whom you can't afford to be friendly.

That afternoon Craig went down to the stockyards to draft cattle. From the window Alison caught glimpses of him as he rode amongst the black mass of steers. She could see the dust rising, hear the crack of a stockwhip above the barking of dogs and lowing of cattle. Nothing would have pleased her more than to slip a saddle and bridle on Banner and gallop down to the stockyards to help, but she knew there were duties here at the house. The children would be coming in from school. There was a pile of ironing waiting in the big Ali Baba basket in the laundry, empty cake tins in the cupboard.

Mary had moved Mrs Carter down to the living room and settled her in a low wing chair. 'Now this is much better,' Mrs Carter observed with satisfaction. 'I hate being shut away in the bedroom and I can keep the old leg up on a cushion just as well out here. It will save you girls running after me all the time too. Craig will tell you I'm just moving down because I can't bear to miss anything that's going on. He might be right at that, but it isn't every day I have two nice girls to talk to—or Craig either. If only it wasn't for——' She broke off on a sigh. 'Oh well, there's no sense in worrying about things you can't do anything about.' Reluctantly she picked up a shapeless piece of knitting. 'Suppose I'll have to do a bit of this, but it's so frustrating. I'm sure the folk who invent knitting patterns deliberately make them difficult to follow. Look at this, Mary,' she regarded the work distastefully, 'did you ever see such a mess?' She jerked angrily at a gaping hole that promptly ran down the rows of stitches.

Mary took it from her. 'If you don't mind my helping——'

'Take the darned thing and fix it for me, will you?'

'I'll have to undo it from the beginning.'

'I don't mind.'

Mary's tone was puzzled. 'What exactly is it supposed to be?'

'A suit for a toddler. These are the pants, believe it or not.'

Mary was carefully unravelling the shapeless piece of knitting. 'If you could start over again using smaller needles? I could help you if you'd let me?'

'Let you? My dear girl, I'd be delighted. I wouldn't have started the wretched thing except that I promised my niece I'd do it. It will never turn out looking like it's supposed to, they never do. I just keep on hoping and trying.' An expression of delight crossed Frances Carter's face. 'But if you did it? I mean, who's to know?'

Mary smiled her slow smile. 'It's a thought. Then you'd be free to concentrate on your Maori proverbs.'

'Now,' said Mrs Carter happily, 'you're talking. Pass me my pad, will you?'

Alison, coming into the room with a cup of tea, made to place it on a low table when a photo album fell to the floor. 'Sorry.' She picked up a coloured picture and found herself looking into Craig's smiling face. How strange to see him in evening dress and how tall and attractive he looked. Her gaze moved to the girl at his side ... strong features, a flashing smile.

'That's Craig and Jo,' Frances was saying.

'Jo?' Something stronger than herself prompted Alison to say quickly. 'Is he—are they——'

'Oh no, they're not serious about each other, not any longer.' She broke off. 'At least, I hope not. It's all over as far as I know—but then,' she grinned rakishly, 'mothers are always the last to hear of anything in the romantic line from their sons. Oh, they'll run on for hours about some deadly dull thing like top-dressing paddocks or the price of mutton, but ask them anything about girl-friends and they'll clam up immediately. I've given up trying long ago.'

Mary came to Alison's side to peer over her shoulder. 'Looks as though it was taken on board ship.'

'It was,' Frances told her, 'the *Oriana*. Craig had gone over to England on a study course, brushing up on wool markets, buyers in all parts of the world, all sorts of business I never can get the hang of. Then on the way back from London he met Jo. She's nice enough in her own way when things are going along just as she wants them, but she'd never make a sheep farmer's wife, not in a hundred years. She stayed with us for quite a while just after she and Craig arrived back in this country. Almost a year ago now, it was.

'Not a great success, actually. It turned out she was much more at home on board ship with all the parties and dancing and fun than she was on a way-back sheep station. She was a city girl and she hated everything about the country from the start, especially the isolation. But she liked Craig a lot, so she set about trying to make him give up the land and put his capital into a tourist motel in a fashionable beach resort up the coast. Can you imagine Craig in that setting? I could have told her at the beginning she hadn't a hope, that you can't push Craig into things, it only makes him go the other way. Anyway, she didn't have a chance of changing his ideas. He's a born man of the land, a *tangata whenua* as the Maoris say. But she gave it a good try, I'll give her that. Three months she stayed with us and she never let up for a moment.'

She chuckled. 'She never got any forrarder either! She even asked me to put in a word on her side about making Craig give up the station property. I told her straight that I haven't been able to make Craig do anything he didn't want to since he left boarding school, and that's quite a few years ago. Not that she didn't try other methods too. She could wheedle anything she wished for out of her parents and she can be quite charming when it pleases her, but even that didn't work. All that charm didn't make a scrap of difference to Craig. Sometimes,' Frances mused, 'I wondered if he really cared enough to make sacrifices. Anyway, one night they had a blazing row and the next morning Jo left the house saying she was never coming back. It was shortly after that that Craig decided to sell out and move up to the north, and the last I heard of Jo was that she had got herself a position as hostess on a cruise ship and had gone away on a world cruise lasting about six months. Shove the picture back in the album, will you, love? It doesn't matter where, it's out of date now anyway. At least, I hope it is. I did hear a rumour that she'd met someone on the cruise ship, an Australian, and they were expected to team up together. Perhaps they're married by now.'

Alison, pushing the picture out of sight between the pages, found herself echoing Mrs Carter's wish.

That night at dinner the two children were subdued and

clearly on their best behaviour. Both left their plates clean.

Mrs Carter, the tea tray balanced on her ample thigh, was delighted. 'They never eat their veges without a fuss as a rule,' she told Alison. 'It must be the way you cook them, so green and appetising. They're good kids really.'

'Good!' exploded Craig. 'Can't you see they're putting on a show, hoping they won't cop it for what they did to Mary this morning?'

Mary said, repressing a shudder, 'It wasn't all that bad.'

'Just a weta crawling around on your pillow.' Craig's tone was grim. 'If ever I catch you kids at that trick again I'll dock your pocket money for a month and cancel the order for those two ponies that are due to come along around Christmas time. Bad enough if it had been Alison, but to pick on Mary——'

Alison felt a stab of resentment. What was so special about Mary? The other girl was looking mystified.

'Why me?'

'Ask yourself! Alison's a country girl, it sticks out a mile. It would take more than a couple of wetas to throw her.'

Her heart lifted on a wave of relief and her bright smile flashed. 'I'm not all that fond of them, especially walking around my pillow. Yuck!'

'What sort of things are you scared of Alison?' queried Patrick with his deceptively innocent gaze. 'Spiders? I know where there's a——' The childish tones died away beneath Craig's warning look.

Presently as the two girls were clearing away the dinner dishes a loud knock sounded on the door, and a few moments later Craig came back into the room accompanied by two men. Tall and powerfully built with dark eyes, the two men were obviously brothers, although one appeared much younger than the other.

'Mate Vasanovich,' the older man introduced himself, 'and this is my young brother Nick.' Soon everyone was talking at once. Alison mused that the one named Nick had a pleasant face and a warm smile, but she wished he would lift his gaze from her face. His obvious interest in herself was becoming a trifle embarrassing. It was a relief to hear Mate say, 'If you're ready, Mary, we'll get cracking right away. Mama's pretty impatient waiting at home. She's in a hurry to catch up with all the family news.'

Mary said with a smile, 'If we are family.'

'Either way we'll have fun sorting things out,' said Mate with his booming laugh. 'You coming, Nick?'

Reluctantly his brother moved with him towards the door. 'Be seeing you ... Alison.' The lingering backward glance he tossed over his shoulder lent meaning to the commonplace phrase.

It was late when Mary returned to the house. As she tiptoed into the bedroom Alison switched on the bedside lamp. 'Had a good time?' she asked sleepily. Then, becoming aware of Mary's air of subdued excitement, 'You did, I can see by your face.' She sat up in bed blinking a little, hands clasped around her knees. 'How did you get on? Were they really your own people?'

Dropping to the end of the bed, Mary pulled a comb from her hair and the long black strands tumbled around her shoulders. 'In a way.'

'How do you mean, in a way?'

'Oh, they were relatives, but only by marriage. Someone's aunt married an uncle of mine.' She seemed abstracted. 'Connections, they call it, don't they?'

Alison was fully awake now. 'All the better! Won't your grandfather be pleased at that news! Now you can get married any time you like. You can take your pick! Or didn't you like the Vasanovich men?'

'Oh, I liked them all right, especially Tony.'

'Tony?' Alison queried.

'He's one of the older brothers. Trained for years to be a lawyer and got all his qualifications. Now he's given it all up to come back to the land with the others. Tony's really something, I could like him a lot, but marriage is out, even if it did happen by some wild chance that things worked out that way. It just wouldn't be possible, not for me.'

Alison looked puzzled. 'Why ever not? Don't they like

80

you, the family? I suppose they made you feel an outsider, a stranger who's trying to burst in on the clan?'

Mary stared at her. 'They were just the opposite. They just couldn't have made more of a fuss of me! You've no idea. Talk about a family gathering! There were relations from Dargaville and all over the district. So many people in the room you could scarcely move. Anyone would have thought I was visiting royalty, the way they treated me. And the supper—I've never seen so much food laid on for a social gathering. The wine was flowing too, heady stuff. Papa Vasanovich makes it himself. He told me he adds extra sugar to make it more potent, and I can well believe it. By the way, the young one, Nick, kept asking me about you—where you came from, how long you're staying here. He's going to ring you, he said. I think he got extra interested after I told him that you do all the cooking around here. The parents were nice, awfully kind; they kept asking me to move over there and stay as long as I liked.'

'What did you say?'

Mary laughed. 'Told them to ask me again in a month when Craig's mother is on her feet again, if they still want me around by then.'

'Thank heaven for that!' Alison breathed a sigh of relief. She had all at once realised how much she would miss Mary were the other girl to move away.

'They told me,' Mary was saying, 'that they'll move away to a small house in Dargaville once the boys are married——'

'Oh, they've got hopes, then?'

'Hopes! I got the feeling they had me lined up for the altar already! Especially the old grandmother——'

'Grandmother!' Alison burst into a peal of laughter. 'What has she got to do with it, even if she has ideas of matchmaking?'

'Matchmaking is a mild way of putting it.' Mary was slipping out of her garments and donning cool cotton pyjamas. 'I guess you can't blame her altogether. She told me that she came out to New Zealand as a mail-order bride

81

herself. The marriage was arranged long before she ever set foot in the country. Marriageable girls were scarce up here in the gumlands in those days.'

'They still are,' Alison remarked smilingly.

'Unfortunately.'

'Unfortunately?' Alison settled back against the pillows. 'You've got to be joking. I still can't see why you're so upset about the grandmother and her marriage-making plans, if it's true.'

'It's true all right. You didn't see the way she was looking at me all evening, sizing me up. I could just about feel her mind ticking over, imagine her saying to herself, "Now here's a nice marriageable girl for one of our men. Yugoslav too, or near enough." I could tell exactly what she was thinking. Would this girl make a good wife? Can she cook a man-sized meal? And those slim hips, not the best for child-bearing. You should have heard the questions she asked me! Why wasn't I married by now? Had I any special man in view? All that stuff. Oh, Grandmother Vasanovich doesn't dodge around a subject, she asks you things straight out!' Her eyes twinkled. 'And she got some straight answers!'

A glimmer of mischief lighted the sleepy eyes. 'Maybe I should have invented a conveniently absent fiancé just for self-protection. I'll need something in that line if I'm going there again. I got the feeling all the time I was there that they're determined to make me one of the family, one way or another. I'm sure they're longing for an excuse to put on a big party with me as the star, and invite their relatives. It wouldn't surprise me,' Mary added wryly, 'if they hadn't arranged for their own band to play at the wedding already. It would be a chance for them all to wear their national costumes and dance all night. Never mind about the bride. Any nice girl would do.'

Alison burst into laughter. 'You're dreaming it all up! Anyway, supposing the grandmother did happen to be looking you over as prospective wife material for one of her grandsons, what does it matter?'

'Matter? You haven't met her! In that family there's

only one head of the tribe, and guess who it is? What she says goes. You can tell that just by meeting them.'

'Oh well,' Alison offered mildly, 'it couldn't make any difference to you, how could it?'

'You'd be surprised at the difference it could make!' Mary's voice was low and tense. 'Even if, I'm just saying *if*, I got to like one of those Vasanovich men and he wanted to marry me, how could I be sure that he really wanted me for myself? That he wasn't just doing what suited the family?'

Alison's lips twitched. 'I guess you'd just know, you'd feel——'

'Perhaps.' Mary's tense look faded and she slipped between the sheets. 'What on earth are we arguing about?' She slanted Alison her crinkly-eyed smile. 'The trouble with this place is there are too many bachelors, and girls are like gold-dust.'

'I know,' Alison agreed happily. 'Fun, isn't it?'

The thought drifted with her into sleep. She was glad she'd come here in spite of Craig Carter and his annoying habit of delving into her personal life.

She was awakened at some time through the night, alerted by an unfamiliar sound—a scraping from somewhere in the house. Could one of the twins have woken up and decided to explore the house in the early hours? As she fled along the passage she glimpsed a light still burning in the small room Craig called his office, but the slight noise seemed to emanate from somewhere at the opposite end of the house. A swift peep into the children's room showed two dark heads on the pillows. Then the noise came again and she decided it must be in the lounge. Flinging open the door, she pressed the switch and light streamed into the room, pinpointing a woodbox beside the open fireplace, a box that was apparently moving along the floor of its own accord. Even as she approached it, however, a furry animal leaped out, making for the fireplace, and a moment later a bushy tail disappeared up the chimney.

It was the sound of footsteps that made her swing around, coppery curls tumbling around her forehead. Craig too was eyeing the soot falling from the chimney.

'A possum. It must have come down the chimney from the big apricot tree outside. I'll get a gun.' Already he had turned away. 'You go outside and keep an eye on him. This is one year the possums aren't going to get away with stripping that tree. The Vasanovichs warned me about that.'

All at once Alison was conscious of shortie-pyjamas and tousled hair. Oh well, he didn't seem to *see* her as a person, his mind was on the possum. He was always giving orders —'Don't walk on the fence', 'Go outside and keep an eye on him', do this, do that. Nevertheless she went to the front door and wrenched it open. Outside moonlight silvered sloping lawns and flowering shrubs. She stood still gazing up at the spreading tree close by. Surely that darker patch of shadow high above was moving.

'Is he still up there?' Craig hurried towards her, rifle in hand, and she wrenched her mind back to the marauding possum. Had the dark patch melted away under her eyes? Now she could see no specially dark shadow amongst the high branches with their hanging fruit. Or was it that she was finding it hard to concentrate, something to do with the disturbing nearness of the man at her side? There was something about him that threw her into a tizzy. She would have to take herself in hand and do something about it, *if she could.*

'Too late!' He was still scanning the big tree. 'He's got away.'

Alison felt sneaky sympathy for the possum. 'If you like I'll get a ladder in the morning and pick all the ripe fruit, beat the birds and ... the ... possums.' Her voice died away and something seemed to be happening to her pulses. It was the silence. She could feel him looking down at her and even in the moonglow she could swear that his mouth had that quizzical twist. His mouth ... his lips ... He bent and kissed her full on the mouth. She had never known a kiss could be like this. The star-ridden sky seemed to ex-

84

plode in sudden radiance and it was quite a time before she could concentrate on his deep tone. 'That's for helping.'

His voice wasn't dictatorial any more, but husky and sort of ... loving. Was it the moonshine that made his eyes so dark and brilliant? She murmured unsteadily, 'I didn't do anything.'

'You did, you know.' Abruptly he released her. He said in an odd tone she couldn't interpret, 'Better go inside, Alison.'

It was only later, on the verge of sleep, that she wondered what it was Craig had been referring to. Did he mean her helping out with Frances? Or the possum? What odds, the wild sweet excitement stayed with her. All that mattered was that he did like her after all.

CHAPTER SIX

In the morning Alison was up and about early, but Craig had already left the house. She caught a glimpse of him mounted on one of the station hacks, riding over a ridge. Now she was free to ride Banner. What bliss to take saddle and bridle from the harness shed and be off over the paddocks! She wouldn't use her own saddle, it might pinpoint her as a show-jumper. A few minutes later she was carrying the riding gear from the stables and climbing the rise towards the paddock at the back of the house.

The mare saw her coming and nickered softly as she came trotting up to the gate. 'Here's your carrot!' Soon Alison was slipping the bit into Banner's mouth and throwing a fluffy white sheepskin over the broad back. A swift glance towards the hills told her that the boss was out of sight. She put Banner to the gate and the mare gathered herself up and rose effortlessly. Then they were away, racing up sheep-nibbled slopes, clearing seven-barred fences and dropping down on the other side while sheep scattered before them in panic and steers pelted away from the flying hooves, with the wind surging in her ears and the early morning sun gilding the tops of the sandhills.

Exhilarated and for some reason extraordinarily happy, at last she took Banner back to her paddock, brushed her down and with a parting pat, left to attend to more mundane duties in the house like seeing the twins off to school and taking Mrs Carter her breakfast. It was all becoming so routine. Strolling down the tree-shaded path, a bridle jingling from her arm, she mused that it was almost as if she belonged here she felt so much at home. She simply couldn't understand it.

Once back in the house, however, she had little time to dwell on anything but the matter in hand. For the children had no sooner waved her goodbye and gone down to the road below to wait for the school bus than Craig arrived back. She could hear him in his office making telephone calls.

She was alone in the kitchen when he came in, a different Craig this from last night. Now he was wrapped up in his work, involved in timetables for the coming week.

'Hi, Alison, how's breakfast?'

From the sink bench she glanced up to meet his smile— but she need not have concerned herself, she thought wryly. Clearly he wasn't thinking of her or of last night, only of the day's programme. What was a kiss anyway? Aloud she murmured, 'Bacon and tomatoes coming up in a few minutes.'

'Not quite ready? No matter—I'll get back on the blower. I've just got word over the grapevine that the shearers are due over the road today, but there's been a cancellation, so I'll book them up here for tomorrow.'

He was back in a few minutes, helping himself from a big pot of tea and peering into the pan Alison was stirring on the electric range. 'Hmm, smells good—I've jacked up things for an early start in the morning. With a full gang the boys bring their own cook with them, but when it's only a matter of a few stragglers to be shorn, the gang can meal at the house. The old lady'll fill you in about all that.' He was eyeing her hopefully, expectantly. 'Can do?'

'Oh dear, Craig,' Mrs Carter must have excellent hearing, Alison thought, to have caught the words from the dining room, 'It's an awful lot to ask of her, all that extra work. I'm afraid she hasn't an idea of what it means. Working against time as they do, the men drink gallons of tea—and eat! If only I wasn't stuck here out of action.'

'Not to worry.' Just in time Alison remembered that she hadn't let on to Craig how experienced she happened to be when it came to cooking for a shearing gang. Evidently there were only two shearers due to arrive at the shed tomorrow and not the full gang. Sternly she repressed the smile that twitched the corners of her mouth. 'I'll try,' she murmured demurely.

'Sweet corn fritters,' boomed Mrs Carter from the adjoining room. 'That's what I always fall back on for the shearers.

I make piles of them and put them in the deep freeze until they're needed. And are they appreciated by a Maori shearing gang!'

'It's an idea.' Already Alison was switching on the oven elements on the electric range.

'The pressure's on,' she told Mary later in the day. 'A couple of shearers are due to start work in the shed first thing in the morning and that means they'll need gallons of tea and lashings of scones or fritters or sandwiches or what have you for smokos.'

'Smokos?' queried Mary.

'Tea breaks to you. They really work, those men. Wait until you take a look at them in action tomorrow.'

'You're the one who's working,' Mary pointed out as she helped Alison to beat up yet another basin of batter. 'All those mountains of corn fritters! The shearers couldn't possibly eat them all.'

Alison wiped a hand across her hot forehead, leaving a long smear of flour. 'You'd be surprised. We'd better whip up another batch just to make sure.'

Indeed, when at smoko the next morning Mary carried down to the shearing shed a tray laden with a massive teapot, cups, scones and fritters, she realised the need for food to men working in the ceaseless activity of the shed. The strong Maori men with smiling pleasant faces and bulging muscles under black work singlets were working at pressure in the heat of the shed. Sweating shoulders bent, each man grappled with a hefty sheep, slicing steadily through an oily fleece, then the sheep was sent down a chute and another one brought in from the holding paddock outside. Another dark-skinned New Zealander was busy sewing up the great filled bales, marking them with the black stencil indicating the farm from which the wool had come. Even while Mary watched, the noise of the machines stopped and in the sudden quiet the shearers straightened their backs and smilingly greeted Mary.

'How did you get on?' Alison asked her when she returned to the house.

She was wide-eyed. 'It looks so exhausting, working at pressure like that. And the heat! I can see what you mean now about the shearers needing lots of food to replace the energy they're using up in that job——' She broke off. 'There was one thing I couldn't understand, though. Just as I came in the door someone yelled at the top of his voice, "Sixty-nine!", but there weren't that many sheep shorn, so it couldn't have been a tally.'

Alison couldn't suppress the laughter. 'They've got a language all their own,' she explained when she could talk again, 'and "sixty-nine" referred to you.'

'Me?'

'It's the traditional shearers' signal when a woman comes in to the shed. Means something like "watch your language, mate."'

Now it was Mary's turn to laugh. 'So that was it! Gentlemen of the shearing shed! What next?'

On the second day, as suddenly as it had begun, shearing was finished. The big shed, slippery underfoot with the oil of the fleeces, was empty and the two cheerful shearers were paid their wages, then piled their gear on the back of their battered truck and drove away to their next assignment.

Craig came into the house in the afternoon, flipped his sunhat across the room, where it landed on the dresser. 'You need a break, Alison.' He studied her thoughtfully. 'You did say you could ride?'

For once she remembered to school her eager voice, 'A bit.'

'Good. That's good enough for me! I'm driving some cattle over the sandhills today. There's a place over the dunes where I can put them to graze for a while. Care to come along and give me a hand?'

Would she care to do just that? Her heart gave a crazy upsurge and she didn't dare glance towards him for fear he would catch the excitement in her face. Aloud she murmured, 'If you think I can help?'

He nodded. 'That's settled, then.' She might just as well

have been a farm hand employed around the place for all he thought about her personally. 'I've got the steers all ready to shift.' He added carelessly, 'Better bring along your swim-suit and we'll take a dip on the way back along the beach.'

Alison was half way to the door already. 'I'll go and get Banner saddled up.'

'That's my girl!'

Was it the matter-of-fact words that warmed her heart or something in his tone?

She sped past Pedro, Craig's station hack tied to the railings, and soon with the ease of long practice she had saddled her white mare. She was riding down to the house when Mary came hurrying into the yard. 'Alison, wait! a message for you! It came over the phone just now. It's from Nick— you met him the other night with Mate. He's going to a barbecue tonight at a friend's place and wants to take you with him. He's holding the line. Shall I say——'

'You can tell him to forget it!' It was Craig at his most authoritative. Lightly he mounted his horse. 'Alison can't talk to him now. She's giving me a hand with the steers, taking them over the sandhills to the other side. We could be quite a time, mightn't be back until late. You can tell him that too. Got it, Mary?'

'Yes, I guess so, but——'

'Right! We're on our way! See you!' He turned on the rein and wheeled away.

He might have asked me, Alison thought as she fell in beside him, but she didn't really mind. For who could waste time on thoughts of young Nick when one was with Craig? Just being with him put a sparkle into the day.

Presently they were driving the long line of cattle up the slopes. The steers seemed bent on wandering off in all directions, but the dogs were well trained and strays were swiftly brought into line with the heaving black mass. In the clear atmosphere the flack of Craig's stockwhip sang in the air above the lowing of cattle. He hadn't merely been talking, Alison realised, when he had told her he needed help in shifting the steers. Forgetting she was supposed to be an indifferent rider, she was soon galloping off in pursuit of a fleeing black beast or wheeling suddenly to head off a recalcitrant steer. Seated on Banner, she opened one gate after another, and all the while the vast dunes, their drifting sand borne towards them on the prevailing wind, were becoming nearer. After a time they passed by the swan-shaped lake in its teatree setting, but today she had no time to pause to admire the black swans fleeing majestically towards deeper water, nor to seek the source of the perfume of cabbage tree blossom—sweet, pervading, elusive—that filled the air around them.

'Head them off this way!' Craig called, and she urged Banner up a precipitous slope and down the other side while steers hurried ahead and the dogs ran around cutting out stragglers. They were approaching long symmetrical lines of pines, moving on to the sand dunes where marram grass clung to the slopes and the wind was endlessly blowing. The drifts of sand were deeper now, slowing down the pace of horses and steers as they plodded over hot sand. Already Alison's eyes were stinging and her hair felt gritty from the blowing sand, but she didn't mind one bit, not when she was with Craig, helping him with work she knew and loved. She became aware that he was eyeing her with his engaging grin. 'Thought you told me you weren't an experienced rider?'

'Did I?' She floundered in search of some excuse, came up with, 'It's Banner really. She corners so well, responds to every pull of the reins.'

'Don't be so modest—' At that moment a steer broke away from the milling throng and he sent the dogs to cut it off and bring it back to the moving mass of black beasts. Plodding along in fine sand, they were making slow progress, but somehow Alison was enjoying the ride, sand in her hair and all. At length they reached a ridge and there below was the misty blue of the Tasman, with its wild coastline and endless expanse of sand. Below on the flats she glimpsed an expanse of lush green grass. Even the steers seemed to take fresh heart at the tempting picture below and rushed headlong down the windswept dunes. At last the cattle were herded through gates and penned in grassy paddocks with their long boundaries of tall macrocarpa pines.

Craig had reined in his mount and was busy with the makings. But the task did not prevent him from gazing towards Alison. It was a look she was finding increasingly difficult to sustain. Was it because she was a girl with a secret, or could it be something more personal, an acute *awareness* of him against which she had no defence? She wrenched her mind back to his deep tones. 'We'll take the horses back along the beach. You haven't seen the coast yet, have you?'

She pulled up at his side. 'Not yet. Isn't it supposed to be awfully dangerous?'

He finished running tobacco into the flimsy paper and moistened the cigarette with his lips. 'You can say that again! There's a terrific current running through the main channel. You can see the rip from here.' She followed his gaze to the swiftly-flowing tide. 'Not exactly the sort of sea you venture out on in a small boat—come on, let's go!'

They urged their mounts towards the long line of breaking surf and soon they were moving along the shore, the horses' hooves leaving deep imprints in wet and shining sand.

'The blue penguins nest up there,' Craig told her, gesturing towards high sandstone cliffs at their side. There was nothing to be seen but the tossing sea, and endless expanse of grey-white sand marked with the footprints of innumerable seabirds. The wind was stronger now, salty with the sea tang, and the surf spray blowing towards them was cool and fresh on her face. Funny how she felt so content riding along this lonely shore. They passed by a great bleached log lying submerged in the sand, a sting-ray washed up by the tide, then skirted a crumpled tangle of rusted iron. 'It's an old wreck,' Craig tossed back over his shoulder, 'you'll see them along the coast.'

Indeed as they went on Alison realised that the long expanse of coastline was strewn with bleached timbers thrown up by the sea. A name-plate that had once belonged to a foundered launch, a splintered mast, a rusted anchor protruding from the sand which fortunately Banner caught sight of in time to avert an accident. It was the loneliest place she had ever seen, nothing but sea and sky and sand, yet still the sense of utter content, the deep inexplicable happiness, persisted.

They had ridden some distance along the wet sand when a pile of rocks loomed ahead and Craig urged his mount over the tide-swept boulders. Alison followed on Banner, then pulled rein to look down in surprise at a small sheltered bay. Out of the main current the wind-rippled waters were shining in hot sunshine.

'I thought this would surprise you,' Craig said. 'Look up there.' She followed his gaze upwards to the towering trees that lined the bank, their twisting roots snaking down through the sand. Amongst the leafy branches was a dazzle of fluffy scarlet blossom. 'Pohutukawa's out in flower already. Even for this part of the country, it's early. Let's hope the Maoris aren't right with their saying about early flowering.'

'You mean that we can expect a long hot summer?'

'Meaning one more drought where we happen to live.'

'Maybe it isn't true,' smiled Alison. 'We can always ask your mother about it. She's such an authority on Maori proverbs. She's probably well up in legends and sayings as well.'

He bent on her his warm grin. 'Where do you think I got the story from in the first place? I promised you a swim, remember?'

'I know, I know. I'm so hot and dusty I can scarcely wait to get into that cool water. I brought my swim-suit. I only wish,' she added ruefully, 'I could wash the sand out of my hair.'

'Your hair——' Before she realised his intention Craig reached out his hand. She could feel his touch on the back of her neck, then he was ruffling the blowing copper-red strands. 'Has anyone ever told you——'

Suddenly she was confused. 'Well then, what are we waiting for?' They tethered the horses on a patch of grass and Alison hurried towards the sheltering bushes growing above the bank. It took only a matter of minutes to change into her brief black bikini, but when she ran down to the sheltered lagoon he was already there, clad in swimming shorts. She hadn't realised his splendid physique. He was like a man carved from bronze, slim yet whipcord-strong. Then he was taking her hand in his and they plunged into the salt water that was deep and crystal clear and, after the first breathless instant, delightfully invigorating.

They swam for quite a time, then floated on their backs. It was very still. Relaxed, Alison gazed up into the shining blue dome above.

'Had enough?'

'Okay.'

They splashed through the shallows, then threw themselves down on the warm sand while the sun beat down on them.

Craig's head was dropped on to his crossed arms. Alison stole a glance towards him. The sun was striking lights in his dark hair. He could almost be asleep.

'How come you're so cagey about yourself, Alison?'

She jumped with surprise, then playing for time, she picked up a handful of sand and watched it trickle through her fingers.

'How do you mean?'

'Come on, you know what I mean.'

Such a lazy tone, almost uninterested . . . or was it? 'What —do you want me to tell you?'

He rolled over on his stomach and she caught the quizzical gleam in the dark blue eyes. 'Whatever you want. Anything, everything! Oh, I know,' as she made to speak, 'you've been in the country before and you can ride a bit. A bit! And kindly mind your own business, Craig! Is that it?' Even without looking up she was disconcertingly aware of his intent glance. 'Anyone would think you had something to hide! Something like a husband?'

'A husband!' The suggestion was so unexpected that she burst out laughing. Or was the laughter born of a sense of relief? 'For heaven's sake, whatever gave you that idea?' Wildly she ran on, 'You'll be saying next that I'm in hiding from the police. What do you think I've done—robbed a bank, or something? I don't know why you've got all these funny ideas about me.'

It seemed he was not to be so easily diverted. 'Just a hunch.' He challenged her with alive, penetrating eyes. 'Your own fault for not being honest with me at the start! Why not come right out with it and admit you've lived on a sheep station before? You didn't turn a hair at laying on meals and all that for the shearers. You know as well as I do that a city girl would have thrown a wobbly at the mere thought of all that.'

She said very low, 'I didn't say I was a city girl.'

'You didn't say anything, remember? But I'll forgive you,' he stretched out his hand and drew a gentle line along her cheek. His touch sent a quiver of excitement darting down her spine. 'I guess you had your reasons.' His voice softened, deepened. 'If there's anything that's worrying you, anything at all, you can trust me.'

'Oh, I know. I know!' She couldn't think clearly for the dizzy happiness surging through her. The next moment the nagging worry began to crowd in on her once again. 'It's nothing,' she mumbled in distress, 'at least——'

Unexpectedly he laid a bronze finger against her chin, raising her face until she was forced to meet his gaze. 'Forget it. No need to spell it out if it worries you all that much.' His smile was warm as a caress. 'I just want you to know that I'm here if you need me.'

She fought the urge to come right out and tell him all she was hiding. And spoil everything? All the brittle happiness she had stumbled on? She forced a smile and said unsteadily, 'You mean, a shoulder to cry on?'

'If you like.'

Why did it hurt so much to keep a still tongue in her

head? He must think she was acting very strangely. Yet to confide in him was unthinkable—him of all men! Because she had to say something to break the silence she murmured very low, 'I was brought up in the country. I've been used to housekeeping on a sheep farm, cooking for shearers and all the rest of it.'

'I get it,' he said, and waited. A question lingered in his eyes. 'Isn't there a bit more to it than that?'

'How could there be?'

'Okay, if that's the way you want it!' Did she imagine the frustration in his tone? Impatiently he sprang to his feet and putting out his hand pulled her up beside him. 'We'd better get cracking.'

All at once she felt helpless, obscurely annoyed with him and angry with herself for being trapped in this impossible situation. She said, 'We won't be back late, then? Maybe I could have made the barbecue after all.'

He threw her an odd unreadable look, said coolly, 'I got the idea we'd had all that out hours ago, decided it was no go.'

She met his eyes defiantly. '*You* decided.'

He stared at her incredulously. 'Are you telling me you wanted to go out with that Nick character?'

Suddenly her throat was tight with defiance and anger. 'I wouldn't have minded,' she said, and slipped away up the bank to the spot where she had left her garments.

They completed the remainder of the journey back to the house in frustrated silence, the horses splashing through the edge of the breakers and the dogs frisking over flecks of sand blowing on the sand while around them along the empty shoreline, sky, water and land seemed to merge together in a pale no-colour blur.

When they had brushed down their mounts and put away the gear Alison preceded Craig into the house. She was still seething with annoyance towards him and in some obscure way, with herself. It had been such a heavenly outing, just the two of them away in the still hot world of the sandhills and then she had to spoil it all. That was the worst of deception, she reflected on a sigh, it got you into all manner of unpleasant situations you hadn't counted on when you started off under another name, even if it did happen to be your own. Was it possible that Craig had a suspicion of the truth? She was such a hopeless nit when it came to lies and evasions. Could it be he really suspected her of running away from all manner of unpleasant things, ranging from theft and a possible prison sentence to an unwanted husband? At the thought she couldn't help giggling to herself. Oh, Craig, if you only knew! But thank heaven you don't! That would really ruin everything between us. Everything? There was nothing between her and Craig, nothing at all. He was hateful, hateful ... questioning her ... trying to make her betray herself ... probing into her personal affairs. By the time she entered the house she had worked herself into an even deeper sense of resentment.

In the kitchen Mary was peeling potatoes. 'Hi, I thought you mightn't be in until late, so I thought I'd get dinner on the way——' She broke off. 'What's the matter? Did all that sand get too much for you?'

Alison pulled herself together and forced a smile. 'No, no, it was wonderful to see. We even had a dip in the sea. It was super...' Until Craig began his enquiries. Did he really suspect her? He seemed to know she had something to hide. She wrenched her mind back to Mary's careless tone. 'Remember young Nick? He came over here with Mate to collect me when I called at their home the other night.'

'Vaguely.'

'Well, he remembers you. He couldn't stop talking about you the night I was there with the family. He's really fascinated by you. He's phoned three times today, hoping you'd get back early by some chance.'

'I told him I couldn't go to the barbecue with him——'

'Don't tell me, tell him! He just wouldn't take no for an answer, said he'd push his luck and call for you around eight anyway, just hoping. I told him I'd pass on the message, but I didn't give much for his chances.'

'You're wrong, you know.' Alison could have laughed at the expression of surprise on Mary's face. 'I can change my mind, can't I——'

'But Craig——'

'Has nothing to do with my affairs.' She rather spoiled the bravado of the statement by adding, 'Anyway, he won't be here. He found a fault in the pump this morning and he's going out down to the gully soon to fix it. He said he wouldn't be back until dark.' And a good thing too. She just knew that given half a chance Craig would prevent her from going out with Nick. He would invent some urgent task, contrive somehow to stop her going out tonight, heaven only knew why, unless ... But he couldn't be jealous of young Nick on her account. It didn't make sense. Unconsciously she sighed.

When she went into the living room she found Craig there with his mother. Frances was telling him how Mary had typed out some pages of the long lists of Maori proverbs she was working on.

'You're lucky, you know,' Craig told her. 'Without the old leg out of action you'd never have found the time to get on with your bits and pieces.'

'Look who's talking!' retorted Frances. 'Without the old leg laid up you would never have had Alison to help you take the cattle over the sandhills today.'

'That's a point.'

But glancing towards his dark inscrutable face Alison got the impression that at this moment the boss wouldn't care where she was so long as she didn't happen to be living right here in his home. And all because she wouldn't, couldn't answer his persistent questioning. For there surely couldn't be any other explanation for his forbidding expression.

Frances' bright brown eyes darted a glance from Craig to Alison. 'So that's how it is, you didn't enjoy your ride over the sandhills today?'

'Oh, but I did!' It was the truth. She had been enjoying it—oh, so much, until ... All at once she became aware of

Craig's enigmatic look and tried to infuse some enthusiasm into her tones. 'It was fantastic.'

Craig was silent and she heard her own voice running nervously on. 'We rode miles and miles over the sand and when we got over the dunes there was this lush green grass with the sea beyond. The view from the top was worth the ride and the sea-breeze blowing on your face was a joy. Just wait until you go there!'

'I will, one of these days,' Frances said. 'What did you do then?'

It was Craig who answered. 'Came back along the beach and had a swim in the bay.'

Mrs Carter's glance rested on her son's set face. 'You don't seem very excited over your first swim of the season.' She grinned her rakish grin. 'Maybe it's just a case of "*ma roto hoki kia ora ka paite korero*".'

'Goodness, whatever's that?' Alison spoke absently. She was still acutely conscious of Craig's firmly-set mouth.

'What she's trying to get through to you,' came his sardonic tones, 'is "put the kettle on".'

'I get it.' Alison moved towards the electric jug. 'Even if I never ever learn another Maori proverb, I'll have to remember that one.'

'That's only Craig's interpretation,' his mother told her. 'What it really says is, "if the inner man is refreshed the conversation will be agreeable".' She was looking at Craig, who had moved to the window and was staring out towards the sheep-threaded hills. He said grim-lipped, 'I wouldn't bet on it.'

When dinner was over and the children safely tucked up in their beds, Alison hurried away to get ready for the evening ahead. A quick shower, a light dusting of powder on cheeks still slightly warm from the effects of the hours spent out on the sandhills during her afternoon ride with Craig. For a moment she stood motionless facing the mirror. Craig ... why couldn't she get him out of her mind?

CHAPTER SEVEN

PRESENTLY she was ready for the outing, cool and fresh in an embroidered muslin dress that swirled around her ankles, white sandals on her feet. The coppery curls she had tamed into waves with only a few rebellious tendrils escaping around her forehead.

At that moment the doorbell rang and Mary went up the hall to answer it. As Alison came out of her bedroom she caught the eager boyish tones. 'Evening, Mary! Tell me, is Alison back yet?'

Alison went along the hall to meet him. 'Right here! How are you, Nick?'

'Fine—now.' There was a warm glow in the dark eyes, and glancing up at him Alison realised that Nick had taken infinite pains with his appearance. The thick black hair was brushed and shining and around him she caught the perfume of after-shave lotion. 'You're coming!' There was no doubting his expression of incredulous delight at sight of her. Indeed it seemed he couldn't take his eyes from her face. 'Gee, it's my lucky night!'

'Think so?' She turned away with a smile. 'I'll just go and say goodnight to Mrs Carter.' When she returned Mary was chatting with Nick. 'You should come along with us,' Alison suggested to the other girl, and was aware from a corner of her eye of Nick's transparent expression of dismay.

Mary waved the invitation away with a lift of her hand. 'Some other time, maybe. I'm busy here tonight, and be-sides——' Alison saw Nick's boyish face relax. 'Run along you two.' And to Nick, 'Take care of her.' A serious note threaded the light tones. 'I'm giving you fair warning. If anything happens to Alison you'll have to answer to the boss.'

Nick flung himself around. 'What's it to him?' he asked sharply.

'Nothing, nothing,' Alison said quickly. 'What Mary's getting at is that Craig's all on his own on the place and I can lend him a hand outside. You know? Mustering, boundary riding, all that stuff. I was brought up on a sheep farm.' Careful, Alison, don't let yourself get too carried away. 'I guess,' she said with an odd little pang, 'he's just got used to having me around.'

Nick looked relieved. 'If that's all there is to it. Don't worry,' he grinned towards Mary, 'I'll take good care of her. Have to,' he added with boyish candour. 'I've borrowed my brother's new car for the night.'

'Borrowed?' Mary flashed him her glimmering secret smile.

'Sort of. He just doesn't know about it yet,' Nick admitted. 'I thought it was safer to do it this way. Tony's a bit particular about who he lends his car to. He's away some where tonight, catching up with someone he knew in town. I'll let him know tomorrow, if he happens to ask. That's what comes of being the eldest of the family,' he explained to Alison with a grin. 'Tony gets the best of everything. He was the one who was sent to town for a college education. He went through university and came out of it with a degree in law. He was in practice in the city for ages, that's how he came to afford a car like the one I've got tonight, then what does he do but throw it all up and come back to join the rest of us on the farm! Not that he isn't a heck of a help when it comes to keeping the books and records, and we could do with an extra hand around the place—guess he's told you the story, Mary? You two seemed to have a lot to talk about the other night?'

'That's right.' For the first time Alison saw Mary uneasy and clearly at a loss for words. Why, she was actually colouring, Mary who had always seemed so coolly in command of her emotions. Could she and Tony possibly—She shook the thought away.

'You say Tony's away seeing someone?' Mary was speaking diffidently, as though the words were being dragged from her lips. 'I didn't know,' she said very low, 'that Tony had a special girl-friend.'

'Old Tony—a girl-friend!' Nick broke into a chuckle. 'If he has he keeps her pretty well hidden away. No, you're way off beam there. A guy from town called him up and they took off for a day's shooting further up country.'

'Oh, I see.' Could this be Mary, marvelled Alison, with this swift change of mood? For now her eyes were shining and even her voice was different, light and happy. 'I just wondered.' The next moment she was back to the placid-natured girl Alison had come to know. 'I'll see you off.' Opening the front door, she peered outside, taking in the long red car illuminated in the light from the passage. 'So that's Tony's car. It's awfully opulent-looking, isn't it?'

'It's a beaut!' Enthusiasm rang in his tones. 'I took her out for a burn the other night, got away with it while Tony was out. On the open road you can really put your foot down. You wouldn't believe the speed I hit——' Catching Mary's glance, he broke off. 'It's okay, I told you I'd take good care of Alison.'

'You'd better,' warned Mary. 'I don't envy you facing up to Craig if any harm came to her.'

'Goodness, what is all this?' Alison broke in with a teasing smile. 'We're only going to a barbecue, not a speedway meeting. Come on, let's go!'

Outside an amethyst haze lay over the hills. There was no sound but the melancholy lowing of the steers. As they strolled down the drive Nick sent her a warm sideways glance. 'Gee, you look great!'

'Thanks.' But she wasn't really listening. She was scanning the shadowed scene in search of Craig. She should be relieved that he hadn't yet returned to the house, yet somehow she wasn't. For what satisfaction was there in gaining a victory over one's opponent when the enemy wasn't at hand to be made aware of his defeat?

Soon they were seated in the shining vehicle, lurching down the winding path from the house. She slipped out of the car to open gates and close them again and presently they were on the curving grey metal road where raw cuttings slashed the darkened hillsides. As they sped on shadows lengthened in the blue dusk and tops of cabbage trees were black spears cut sharply against the lemon afterglow of sunset. She suspected that Nick was engrossed in the powerful car he was driving, enjoying the sensation of speed.

'Where are we going?' she asked.

'Turner, the name is. It won't take long to get there. It's not far.'

She threw him a laughing sideways glance. 'Like ten miles?'

'Eleven, actually.'

Dust rose behind them as they sped on, car lights sweeping in an arc over the road ahead and playing over dust-coated bush. She caught a swift glimpse of lake waters at the side of the road, then they were moving on at speed, sweeping between banks of tall tea-tree sombre in the shadows.

Presently they fell into a companionable silence. She suspected that to Nick having her here with him was sufficient to make the evening a success. As for herself, the adoring sideways glance he sent her every now and then was comforting to her battered ego. Now had it been Craig who had been her companion tonight probably by now, in that disturbing way of his, he would be shooting questions at her. Questions to which she had no answers, or at least none that she could confide to him. Why was she thinking of him all this time anyway? To divert her mind she said to Nick, 'How come you haven't got a car of your own?'

For a moment he was silent. 'I—well ... thing is I had a prang a couple of weeks ago, put the car out of action. It was a bit of a write-off.'

She was only half listening. 'You weren't hurt in the crash?'

'Good grief, no! I'm used to them, I guess. It was the old jalopy that let me down, but,' his tone lightened, 'I'm picking up another one next week, an English job.' She knew by his animated tone that she had sparked off a subject that promised to keep him happily engrossed for some time, leaving her free to pursue her own thoughts.

Darkness had fallen when at last they rounded a curve and came in sight of a ranch-style house set high on a rise. Lights streamed from wide-open doors and windows and wisps of smoke were rising from a flare-lighted enclosure in the shelter of tall trees. Nick sped up the winding driveway and soon they were being warmly welcomed by a group of young people who came hurrying towards them. 'You're just in time, Nick!' In the chatter and laughter she failed to catch the various names, but there was no doubting the warmth of the welcome extended towards her. Clearly in numbers the men far outnumbered girls, and she wondered if that could be the reason why she was suddenly in such demand, everyone pressing her to glasses of wine or dips or tiny savouries.

Presently they all moved to a grassy spot sheltered by high native trees, tea-tree and ferns. Smoke was rising from a barbecue area where benches and long wooden tables were set out on the grass. The girls had brought bowls of rice, salad and garlic bread and the men were soon busy cooking lamb chops, sausages and potatoes in foil. Later someone plucked at a banjo and voices rose in the songs of the day. All at once in a silence a guitar sobbed out a haunting Maori melody that brought a mist to her eyes. Was it because it made her think of Craig . . . always Craig?

'What's wrong?' Nick, his young face flushed from the heat of the glowing coals, came hurrying towards her.

She put on her brightest smile. 'It's the guitar music. It always does things to me.'

Nick nodded. 'I know what you mean. He's not bad, Kevin. Never had any lessons either.' His gaze went to a young man whose fair head was bent over the guitar. 'He's a natural—hey, what would you like to eat? Chops? Steak? Sausages? Just say the word. Don't be put off by the look of the bananas. They may look repulsive, but with a dab of ice cream and brandy poured over them you'd be surprised how good they are!'

'It doesn't matter. Just bring me something—anything, I don't mind.' Alison knew it would be difficult to force herself to eat the food. Somehow for her the evening wasn't going at all well and it was all her own fault. She stood in the shadows, only half aware of the chatter and laughter echoing around her. It wasn't Nick's fault that right from the start she had been conscious of a heaviness of spirit she couldn't understand. Why couldn't she enjoy herself here like the others? She was away from household chores with Mary well able to see to Frances, and the twins if need be. She should be feeling as free as the air—yet perversely her mind kept reverting to the house on the hill. Craig would be back there now. What would be his reaction to her taking off to enjoy herself, defying his orders and doing what she pleased instead of meekly agreeing to his demands? Enjoying herself? Of course she was, in a way. *You're not and you know it. Without Craig everything seems deadly flat, to have no real meaning.* Even when he's being overbearing and demanding he still makes life ... interesting. Nothing seems to register without him. I wish I were there to see his face when he finds out that I've gone out with Nick. Anyone would think he was violently jealous of young Nick. I wish he were. I wish he cared enough for me to be jealous. Where were her thoughts leading her? She couldn't love him—or could she? The truth came with devastating impact. To think she had really imagined that she could make her own way, plan her life the way she wanted it. *The way she wanted it!* Now she had fallen in love, deeply, irrevocably, hopelessly with a man who regarded her as no more than a help on the farm. Worse, with a certain degree of suspicion. The stern lines of his face came back to her. Oh, she should have known, that first kiss should have told her what was happening. A kiss that he had no doubt already forgotten.

I wish I could forget. No, I don't. I wish he would care for me, love me, so that when I confessed to him who I

105

*really am, he'd trust me, believe me when I explained to him
that coming to his home was a sheer accident, that I had no
idea it was his property that day I walked in with Mary.*

'Don't you like it here?' Nick's anxious tones jerked her
from her reflections. His soft dark eyes regarded her with
concern. 'They're a good crowd really. They won't mind if
you're a bit shy.'

Shy! If only that were the reason for her lack of anima-
tion..Evidently she wasn't very skilful at disguising her feelings for some time later, though the gathering showed no
sign of breaking up for hours yet, Nick whispered: 'Had
enough? Shall I take you home?'

She nodded agreement and with a murmured farewell to
their hostess they slipped away to the car. It was funny,
Alison mused as they shot down the winding drive and
lurched into the dark deserted road, that she didn't much
care how fast they travelled so long as she was going back to
Craig, besotted idiot that she was! Lost in aching longing,
she was scarcely aware of the fragment of road unfolding
ahead in the glare of the headlamps as they sped up dark
slopes and hurtled down again on the other side. After
travelling along a flat road for some distance they approached a cone shaped hill. They were nearing the top of
the rise when she became aware of a continuous blaring
from a car horn from somewhere in the darkness ahead.

'Nick, stop!' A premonition of danger sharpened her
tone. 'Slow down, *please*!' But it was too late. They swept
over the top of the hill straight into the midst of cattle milling over the roadway. The crashing of metal echoed above
the frantic lowing of steers as the car was jolted to a violent
stop and Alison felt herself flung forward. The safety belts
saved them, she realised a moment later, from being flung
out on to the road. She could feel the trembling of Nick's
arm against her own, hear his distressed cry, 'Alison! Alison! Are you all right?'

'Yes, yes!'

Still he kept repeating the words, seemingly not able to
take in her answer. Dazedly she realised that another car

was approaching, pushing its way forward between the groups of terrified cattle moving over the roadway. A few moments later the vehicle was pulling up beside them and Craig was leaping out, wrenching open the door of the crumpled car. 'Alison!' His tones were hoarse with feeling. 'You're not hurt?'

'No——'

'If you only knew what it means to me to hear that, my darling——'

'She's okay, we both are.' Nick appeared to have recovered his wits. 'It's the car——'

'To hell with the car!' She had never heard Craig's voice so harsh and forbidding. 'Didn't you hear my warning?'

Nick said uneasily, 'There was something——'

'Only you were going too fast to pull up in time *with Alison in the car with you*!' Roughly he jerked him forward. 'Get out!'

'Take my car,' he rasped. 'Stop at the first house you come to and rustle up a couple of men. Tell them to bring dogs with them and torches and to get up here *fast*!'

'Can do. I'll come back and give you a hand with the stock.'

'*You!*' Craig's scathing tone implied a cold contempt for the younger man. He bent to take a flashlight from his car. 'I'll patrol the road until the others get here. Now *get going* before there's another smash-up!'

Nick said, shamefaced, 'I'm on my way. Coming, Alison?'

'No!' Craig's tone brooked no argument. 'Alison stays here with me! I'm letting you have my car, but I'm not trusting you with Alison. Not now—or ever. Get it?'

Without another word Nick stumbled towards the car and got behind the wheel. Headlamps of the turning vehicle pinpointed two badly injured cattle lying nearby, then lighted the shattered glass on the road and the other car slewed around at an angle, its bonnet crumpled. As Nick slowly moved amongst the panicky cattle she had a moment's apprehension. What if he were more affected by the

107

accident than he realised? 'Do you think he'll make it?'

'He'd better.' Craig's tone was grim.

'He didn't know you were trying to warn him.'

'He should have—I made it plain enough. Anyone else would have pulled up long before that after I gave the alert instead of trying to prove to you how fast his car would go.'

'I'm sure it wasn't that.'

He ignored that. 'Here's hoping,' he said grimly, 'the next guy who shoots over the hill has a bit more sense.'

'Nick didn't *know*——'

'Your friend,' he pointed out, 'is lucky to be alive. Taking risks with you right there in the car with him! Don't ask me to feel any sympathy for him. He deserves all he gets, and more!' All at once his voice was gentle. 'Don't worry, I'll get someone to run you home.'

'You won't, you know.'

He was talking to her as though she were a child with no mind of her own. Maybe the full effects of the crash would hit her later, but meantime she had no intention of allowing herself to be meekly ordered back to the house. For she knew, who better, that Craig would need all the help he could get in rounding up the steers now moving towards the dark bush at the side of the road.

'I'm staying here to help,' she told him firmly.

'Good for you!' A reluctant appreciation tinged his voice. He added on a sigh, 'If only I could be certain you're fit enough to do the job.'

'Try me!'

For once she had an advantage over him. She knew he had little time to argue, for another vehicle might come over the rise at any moment. Before he could make any further comment she had moved to Nick's car and running her hand along the dashboard, found what she sought, a powerful flashlight. All at once she remembered the other guests at the house she had left. With luck they might not yet have left the barbecue and might not be on the road until the danger was past.

'Stay where you are, Alison.' He was bending over an injured steer and the next moment a rifle shot echoed above the lowing of cattle. Another shot followed as Craig put the badly injured beasts out of their misery.

When she came back to his side she said, 'If you like I'll keep watch at the top of the hill.'

'You'll stay right here with me until we get some help. I'm not risking anything happening to you—not again.' As if to emphasise his words he threw an arm around her shoulders, imprisoning her at his side. Alison didn't know whether it was the effect of his nearness or the results of the recent collision that caused her to tremble so violently. How could he help but notice? He did. All at once his voice was low and concerned, 'You're shaking.'

'It's nothing,' she lied. It just went to show the odd way in which shock could affect one, giving rise to ridiculous urges like this longing to fling herself against his hard muscular chest and find safety and protection in his arms.

It seemed an age waiting, each moment filled with dread. Supposing the batteries of the torch failed? Or what if a vehicle moving too fast to brake in time at sight of the warning light caused a second accident?

At last, however, they caught the gleam of approaching car lights as a car moved slowly and carefully up the rise, and taking a zig-zag course through the moving cattle, pulled in beside Craig. In a few terse sentences he arranged for the two shepherds with their dogs to help him and Alison to round up the straying steers. The other two men in the car he posted with flashlights on the road to warn approaching traffic of possible danger.

'That is,' his voice was suddenly gentle as he turned towards her, 'if you still feel up to lending a hand?'

'Let's go!' she said, and soon she was running through the bush with the others as they rounded up the cattle and guided them back through the opening from which they had strayed.

There was a pre-dawn lightening on the horizon and the others had returned to their home when the last black steer had been returned to the paddock. Craig secured the gate.

'Come on, Alison, I'll take you home.' Did she imagine the tenderness in his tone, just as she must have imagined that 'my darling' at the moment he had arrived on the scene of the accident?

He saw her into the car and soon they were moving along the shadowed road. The pale glow in the eastern sky changed and deepend to the shining gold of sunrise. A delightful feeling of relaxation stole over her. She was suddenly sleepy and awfully content. Her head drooped to his shoulder and his arm was around her, warm and tender and infinitely satisfying. She murmured drowsily, 'I thought you'd be angry with me.'

'Angry? With *you*, Alison?'

'You know, about my taking off tonight with Nick. You didn't seem to like the idea.'

His arm tightened around her. 'Not your fault. You weren't to know the reputation he's got for crazy driving.' The hard angry note was back in his voice and she knew that once again she had spoilt the happiness of the moment with her stupid remark. 'He's smashed up car after car and so far he's managed to bale out in time or had the incredible luck to walk out of a crash unhurt—but to hit those speeds is asking for trouble. Not that it isn't what he deserves. But to take risks with *you* in the car. I won't forgive him for that in a hurry!'

Her heart swelled on a wave of elation. He'd been concerned for her safety. That was the reason he had offered resistance to Nick taking her to the barbecue tonight. He'd thought enough of her, been sufficiently concerned to come searching for her. At least, so it would seem. 'How did you come to be there at just the right time?' she asked, and held her breath for the answer.

Craig's eyes were on the road ahead. 'Had a ring from a guy heading for Dargaville, a neighbour a few miles away. He almost collided with a steer along the road himself, knew I leased some land up here and thought they might have belonged to me.'

So—Alison jerked herself up the seat—his concern had

110

been for his stock. Typical! She wrenched her mind back to the deep vibrant tones. 'I can tell you I couldn't get here fast enough. You were on my mind all the way, but I was too late.' He pulled her back close beside him and blissfully she relaxed once again. 'You are feeling okay?' he asked with solicitude. 'No aches and pains, no headaches?'

'Not a thing. I'm fine, honestly!' She hoped he wouldn't guess at the reason for the radiance in her tone.

They drove on in silence and as they reached the entrance gates on the roadway gently he released his arm from around her shoulders. 'You stay put, Alison, I'll do it.' Feeling deliciously cherished and all at once *cared for*, she waited while he opened and closed the wide gates one after another. It was almost worth having been involved in one of Nick's accidents, she mused dreamily, to be treated so tenderly by the boss instead of being merely his Girl Friday.

The eastern horizon was slashed with bars of gold against tumbled crimson clouds as they drove in at the last gate. Craig shut off the engine and came around to her side of the car. 'You've had a rough time tonight.' She was unaware of a cut across her forehead where the blood had congealed, of grazed arms and dust-smeared face. She only knew that he was looking at her with an expression she had never seen in his eyes before. Maybe she hadn't imagined that 'darling' after all.

'Me? I'm all right . . .' Her voice slurred and she seemed to be drifting away on a dark sea of ineffable content. 'Are you taking me home, Craig? . . . Back to . . . Te-o-nui . . .' Her voice trailed away into black folds of oblivion. Then the mists cleared and she was aware of Craig gathering her up in his arms.

'All right now?' He bent his head and she could feel his breath on her face. For a heart-stopping moment she thought he was about to kiss her, then he went striding up the path. At the door he set her gently down. 'I wouldn't have had you hurt for anything.'

Shakily she replied, 'You did try to stop me going out tonight.'

His voice hardened. 'Next time I'll make sure.'

She smiled up into the dark closed face. 'What had you in mind? Locking me up in my room? Keeping me here for ever?'

'I wish I could.' The words were so low she barely caught them. A moment later he pushed open the door and a girl who had been seated on the window seat jumped to her feet. 'Craig! I thought you were still asleep!' Running across the room, she threw her arms around his neck and kissed him on the lips. 'Pleased to see me?'

He didn't appear to hear her. 'What are you doing here?'

'Waiting for you. Aren't you surprised?'

He disengaged the clinging arms. 'Never mind that now. Alison's been in an accident,' he explained briefly. 'We've been quite a time clearing up afterwards.'

'Oh!' The stranger's cool glance raked Alison's dishevelled figure. 'She looks okay to me.' The next minute she was laughing up into Craig's unresponsive face, chattering on without pausing for breath.

So this, thought Alison with sickening certainty, is Jo. She had an impression of a round-faced girl with cropped dark hair, pouting red mouth, a full voluptuous body. Alison wrenched her mind back to the strong assertive tones. 'I came the moment I got to hear about your mother being laid up. I knew she'd be needing me to help out and I wasn't going to let her down. I'd just got home when I heard the news and I made arrangements to come north right away. What do you know? I happened to run into a friend who was motoring up this way to her aunt's place for a holiday. We arrived there late last night, so I decided I'd come over here as soon as I could.' A gay ripple of laughter. 'The farmer went out at daybreak on his way to work somewhere miles from here, so I got him to drop me off on the way. I wanted to surprise you only it was me who got the surprise! I thought you'd be coming out to get breakfast and——'

'Pack it up, Jo——' The deep peremptory tones cut across the stream of chatter. Over Jo's head Craig's gaze

112

went to Alison. 'You've done a great job tonight, but you need some sleep now. I'll get you a brandy first, though, something to settle you down. Right?'

She nodded, raising her heavy glance to his face. I'm doing exactly what he tells me to do and all at once it doesn't seem to matter. Now that Jo is back in his life he won't be caring whether or not his Girl Friday goes against his wishes. The curious floating sensation surged over her once again. Somehow the impression of being ignored by Jo was more humiliating than if she had been insulted. Just a nothing person, not even worth a thought. Angrily she lifted her chin, gulped down the drink Craig had handed to her, and made her way to the door. She was only vaguely aware of Jo's sweetly provocative tones. 'You're making me curious. What's so world-shattering about what she did tonight, whoever she is?'

Craig's tone was abrupt. 'Tell you some time.' But of course he would have matters to discuss with the girl he might still care for, things of far greater import to him than herself. At the bathroom door she paused, staring incredulously at the mirrored reflection. Small wonder that Jo had dismissed her as someone beneath her notice. What a mess! Blood smeared across her forehead, the fine muslin of her dress torn and bedraggled. She shook her head and a shower of earth and leaves fell to the floor.

Forcing back the tears that threatened to overflow, she washed away the dried blood from her face as best she could and, thankful that Mary was fast asleep, stumbled into bed.

CHAPTER EIGHT

THE brandy Craig had insisted on her drinking must have made her sleep soundly, because it was hours later when she awoke. Hazily she lay listening to voices echoing from the dining room, then all at once realisation came rushing back. A dull throbbing started over her eyes and a sense of bitter anguish threatened to overwhelm her. Clearly Jo had come here with the intention of making up old differences between herself and Craig, and somehow—Alison swallowed over the lump in her throat—she would have to force herself to get used to the situation. How could she bear to be here, seeing the other two making up their quarrel? Yet she couldn't leave Mrs Carter and the twins to the indifferent care of a girl who was obviously using them as a means to be with Craig. Besides, hadn't she promised Frances she would be her for as long as she was needed, and she sensed that Mary would be leaving the homestead now that Jo had taken up residence here.

And Craig . . . how was she to hide her feelings for him beneath his deep perceptive gaze? But of course he would have no eyes for her, not now. He would have Jo, experienced, travelled, probably an expert in all manner of accomplishments with the single exception of the outside work that came so naturally to herself. And where had it got her? Being his Girl Friday was about as unromantic as being employed as a general hand on the property. Even Frances regarded her first and foremost as Craig's outdoor helper. Only a crazy idiot like herself would ever have allowed herself to dream up a lasting relationship with Craig.

Honestly now, what did she have to go on? A few brief moments of tenderness, light kisses to which—her cheeks burned—she had been all too responsive, a whispered promise in the treacherous moonlight. Add to that a certain male jealousy over young Nick, who meant nothing to her, nothing. When you came right down to it it wasn't much to build a dream on, not half enough.

You've been in love with him ever since that first sight of him, back in your old home, only you wouldn't admit it even to yourself. How could you have been so stupid? You might have known that a man like Craig would have someone else in his life, someone who was older, more experienced in the ways of love. Oh, no doubt he'd meant what he had said to her, *at the time*. An older girl, someone like Mary, would never have allowed herself to be taken in by such trivial incidents. Nor would she be, ever again. She made an effort to be stern with herself. Put it down to experience, forget all about him. But how forget when just to be in the same room with Craig sent her senses spinning wildly, and why did experience hurt so much?

'Coming, ready or not!' Mary thrust her head around the door, then carried a laden tray towards the bed. 'Don't get up! You're supposed to stay in bed all day, boss's orders! My, you were lucky,' she ran on, putting down the tray and crossing the room to draw the curtains, 'not to be really laid up today——' She broke off, taking in Alison's strained pale face. 'You are all right aren't you? You look awful!'

'I'm okay.' Alison forced a smile. 'Such luxury, breakfast in bed! Or is it lunch? After this I'm getting up.'

Mary eyed her ruefully. 'The boss won't like it.'

'Too bad.' To change the subject Alison said, 'Have you heard how Nick is today? He rushed off in a hurry last night. Craig made it fairly clear that he didn't want him back on the scene.'

'I can imagine. I could have let you in to what Craig had against him—driving like a maniac, I mean—but I didn't like to mention it, and then later I wished I had. Not that it would have made any difference to your going with him last night. You're a stubborn thing when once you make up your mind.'

115

'I know. But is he all right?'

'Nick? No real damage, according to his mother. I was speaking to her over the phone and she's hoping that maybe, just maybe, this time he's learned his lesson. Seems he's terribly upset over you being in the smash-up with him. He keeps ringing through to us with messages for you. I told him you were asleep and that's kept him quiet for a while. I don't envy him if Craig happens to answer the call next time.'

Mary dropped down to the end of the bed. 'You're well out of it this morning. If I were you I'd stay right here for the day. Jo's arrived. You know? The girl who Craig nearly married and thought better about. You can understand why when you meet her——'

'Don't tell me. I did meet her last night, just for a minute.'

'Bet she made the most of that minute!'

'She did, rather.'

'Boy, does she order everyone around to suit herself! But she didn't get far, just managed to upset the whole house. The twins have gone off to school in tears, Frances is hot and bothered and thinks she's running a temperature, and Craig's going around looking as though he hates the whole world. I can tell you I'm keeping well out of his way while he's in that mood.'

'Do you think,' Alison schooled her voice to deceptive casualness, 'she'll be staying long?'

'It all depends on Craig, I take it. If she thinks she has a chance——' Why did putting the truth into words make it hurt so much more? Alison wondered. She wrenched her thoughts back to Mary's voice. 'Craig doesn't strike me as a guy who's crazy about being reunited with his lost love. On the contrary.'

That's only because of my being at the house to complicate matters. Mary's cryptic tones cut across her anguished thoughts. 'Something tells me Jo isn't going to like either of us being here. She hasn't got down to getting everything out in the open yet, but when she does——' She

116

threw up her hands in a gesture of resignation. 'I've washed out my one and only presentable pair of jeans and they're drying on the line, just in case I have to take off from here in a hurry.'

Alison pulled herself out of painful imaginings. 'You don't have to rush away just because of her, unless you want to.'

A smile tugged at the corners of Mary's wide mouth. 'I mightn't have much choice, going by what Frances has been telling me about Jo. Seems she isn't one for other women. Frances doesn't imagine Jo's ever had a real girl friend all her life. I gather she just can't stand competition. Not that that means a thing as far as I'm concerned. Craig's a great guy and I like him a lot, but there's another one living not too far from here who rates pretty high with me, not that Jo would know anything about him!' Her teasing glance rested on Alison's pale face. 'But with you it's different.'

Competition, Alison thought hollowly, was scarcely the word for her and Craig's relationship. Girl Friday, dogsbody, general hand, perhaps. Aloud she murmured, 'How do you mean?'

'Can't you guess? I might be way off beam, but the way he looks at you sometimes, the tone in his voice when he's talking to you——'

Alison felt her pulses leap, then settle again. 'You're imagining all that.'

'Am I? You don't imagine that special sort of feeling between a man and a girl. It's something in the air, you can't mistake it.'

If only it were the truth! When Mary had taken away the almost untouched meal Alison went to the bathroom and turned on the shower taps. It took her quite a time to remove traces of earth stains. Then she washed the dust from her hair and towelled it dry, combing the waves into order. When she was dressed in a cool sprigged cotton shirt and blue jeans the bruises on her legs were hidden and even the long cut on her forehead didn't show when she pulled over it a lock of springy hair. If only heartache were as easily put aside!

She was going down the hall when Craig emerged from the doorway of his office and for a fraction of a second their glances met. Her heavy gaze fell away and to her mortification she could feel the hot colour creeping up her cheeks.

'Alison!' He was at her side in a couple of strides. 'Don't look like that! It's not like you think. I can explain ——'

'Don't bother.' The words cost her an effort, but she got them out in a choked voice. She shrugged away his detaining hand on her arm. 'I know about Jo——'

'You don't, you know!' Roughly he swung her around to face him. 'Now look at me, Alison! Will you listen——'

'No, I won't!' Hurt and pain made her fling the words at him. 'Don't tell me, tell Jo——' She wrenched herself free and hurried away, then, aware of his ominous silence, glanced back over her shoulder. He was standing motionless, his brilliant eyes pale and bleak—some trick of the dim light, surely. Why hadn't she noticed before the deep lines etched down each side of his mouth? 'What's the matter?' she asked unsteadily. 'Did you want something?'

'Yes—you!'

She ignored that and went on, knowing that to stay a moment longer would be to undermine all her defences, for the sight of his sombre shadowed face was almost more than she could bear. And why not? She reminded herself; hadn't he good reason to feel ill at ease with herself and Jo right here beneath his roof?

When she entered the dining room she saw at once that Frances was upset. Two bright spots of colour burned through the leathery-brown of her cheeks and she glanced up at Alison with a tense expression. 'Thank heaven you're all right, dear! You're looking awfully pale today, but that's only to be expected after last night. Craig said you met Jo at some unearthly hour this morning?'

'Yes,' she schooled her voice to a noncommittal note.

118

'She was waiting for us when we got back.'

'She tells me,' groaned Frances, 'that she's come here to take care of me! Heaven forbid! Not that she hasn't got her good points, but patience isn't one of them. I pity any invalid who gets "taken care of" by her. I can't stop her, of course. And the twins can't stand her at any price. They came to stay for a couple of weeks while Jo was with us last year—and talk about fireworks! Jo just doesn't understand children one little bit!'

'If you'd like me to go?' Alison heard her own voice, curiously expressionless.

'And abandon me to Jo's tender care? Not to mention the twins! No, no, better wait and see. I don't want to lose my helper,' her smile for Alison was warm, 'or Craig his Girl Friday either, if I can help it.'

A shaft pierced Alison's heart. That was all she was, his farm helper. Another girl would ride with him over the sheep-dotted hills, *if she loved him enough*. It was Jo who would share his name. And to think, she mused with bitter irony, that I already share that name, did he but know. She wrenched her mind back to Frances' worried tones.

'Jo must have heard about my mishap on the bike right after she got back to New Zealand and she's come haring up here on the chance. It's not me that she's worrying about, I'm just the excuse.' Under the stress of emotion Frances seemed to be giving voice to her thoughts. 'It's a good excuse, the old leg. It's been responsible for quite a lot, one way and another. One thing I know, and that is that Jo's set her heart on being Mrs Craig Carter, otherwise she wouldn't be here. And she's the sort of girl who gets her own way, or else.'

'I shouldn't imagine,' Alison heard herself saying in a low distressed tone, 'that Craig could be made to do anything he didn't want to.'

'That's true,' agreed Frances. 'But don't you see, that's just the point. Does he want to? He never let on to me how he felt about Jo. To tell you the truth, I wasn't sorry when they broke up. Two strong-natured people like Jo and

119

Craig aren't likely to get on well together for long. Jo must have seen that for herself by now. All those quarrels and making up don't make for a happy married life, I wouldn't think. Of course I don't know how much feeling there was between them. I was hoping that in these past six months he would have forgotten all about her. Perhaps he has. He doesn't look overjoyed at the big reunion—but then with Craig you never can tell.'

Alison hoped she could hide the sense of anguish that was flooding her once again. Why hadn't Craig made mention to her of Jo? Because he had put her out of his mind or because to speak of the girl with whom he had been deeply involved, still gave him pain? About Jo's feelings there seemed no doubt. How delighted she must have been to learn of Frances' accident, giving her an opportunity to make things up with Craig. Perhaps even— a cold hand seemed to close around her heart—absence had wrought a change in Jo's attitudes and she was now willing to accept marriage on Craig's terms. For how could any girl who was loved by him do otherwise?

'Come in, Jo!' Alison forced her mind back to the present. Frances was sweeping aside a pile of papers from a nearby chair. 'I want you two girls to get to know each other, Jo, this is——'

'We've met.' Jo didn't even give Alison a glance. *It wasn't fair*, she thought hotly. She knew she looked years younger than her age. Blame it on those irresponsible reddish-brown curls that *would* cluster all over her head. But that didn't give Jo the right to treat her as a slightly tiresome child. There was no doubt that in the other girl's estimation she rated about on par with the pet sheep grazing near the hedge outside. 'Craig told me he had someone here to see to the housework. I've met Mary too. She's just travelling around the country, I take it, stopping off here for a night or so on the way up north.'

'A night or so? Goodness no!' Mary had entered the room. Now she perched herself on the edge of the table, swinging long jean-clad legs. The sleepy eyes glimmered

120

with mischief. 'I'm employed to look after Mrs Carter while she's laid up. Didn't Craig tell you?'

'No, he didn't!' snapped Jo crossly. 'I've scarcely seen him to speak to.' Swiftly she covered the slip. 'I mean, with the accident and everything. Then he had to go out ear-tagging steers right after he got home. If I'd known——' she broke off in confusion.

'You'd have come up here just the same,' put in Frances with her rakish grin. 'I can see I'll have to put you in the picture about what's been happening around here.' She went on to explain the details of her recent fall from the motorbike followed by the timely arrival of the two strange girls at the empty house. 'It was fate, that's what I say,' she concluded happily. 'Without Alison and Mary I would have had to go to hospital, and as to the twins—I can't imagine what would have happened to them.'

'Oh yes,' Jo murmured carelessly, 'I heard that Karen and Ben had taken off to Switzerland on a skiing trip. If only I'd been available at the time you were hurt it would have saved everyone so much trouble.'

'No trouble,' murmured Mary with her mocking smile.

Jo, ignoring the interruption, swept on. 'But there's no need for you to worry any more, Frances. Now I'm here I can take over. It's what I want to do more than anything.' Even to her own ears the statement must have had a slightly false ring, for she added hurriedly, 'For you, Frances, I mean. I'd do anything for you. I think it's a great idea, suits you fine, and me too. I mean,' the excited expression in the wide blue eyes lent significance to the words, 'I've got to get my hand in.'

Alison was conscious of an almost physical blow. Oh, she should have known! She had really, but all the time she'd kept hoping. Jo might have circled the world, but she wouldn't have found a man to compete with Craig, as she had no doubt come to realise. *I'll always love him, even knowing about him and Jo. I wish I didn't, but there's nothing I can do about it.* As from a distance she became aware of Jo's dictatorial accents. 'This place could do with

121

a face-lift. I couldn't live in a house with these low ceilings, and the bathroom's archaic. A mauve door with silver fittings and crystal taps, I think. But of course,' she added, 'the main thing is to do what *you* want——'

'Well then,' suggested Frances promptly, 'why not stay on here for a holiday? No need for you to worry about anything else. I know how you've always felt about housework.'

Jo's round blue eyes widened innocently. 'Oh, but I couldn't! I just couldn't! I'd feel such a nuisance. No, I've made up my mind.' She turned to Mary. 'There's no need for you to stay any longer. I'm sure Craig will fix up your wages. Probably,' she added carelessly, 'he'll throw in an extra week's pay in lieu of notice. You must be anxious to get on with your travels——'

Alison intercepted Mary's amused glance. 'Not really.'

Jo looked nonplussed for a moment, then she rallied. 'These relatives of yours you told me about, the ones who live in the district——'

'Not relatives, connections,' Mary pointed out, still in a tone of quiet amusement.

'Connections, then. What does it matter?' A faint flush stained Jo's clear satiny cheeks. 'You could go and stay with them.'

Frances laid a hand on Jo's arm. 'Jo, *please*——'

Jo shook herself free. 'It's all right, Frances, I can handle this. I'm sure,' she went on with a visible effort at self-control, 'that once she understands the position Mary will come to see things my way. It's not as if she's indispensable here, and now that I'm here to take over——'

At last Frances got her say. 'But I can't do without her,' she wailed. 'She's my secretary, or just about. She's been helping me to compile my notes. She types them all out for me and between us we've got my book of Maori proverbs well on the way. Besides,' she announced triumphantly, 'she promised to help Craig with his accounts. He spends hours in the office working on the books, and Mary happens to be a trained secretary——'

'It's all right, Frances,' Mary's composed tones cut across the older woman's apprehensive accents, 'I'll come back and see you whenever you need me and we'll sort out those last few chapters together. Craig can give me his account books if he wants to and I'll work on them while I'm over at the Vasanovichs'.'

'Oh, Mary, *would* you? I feel so awful about your leaving like this. As if we were throwing you out.' Genuine distress tinged Frances' low tones.

'You don't need to,' the mocking smile still played around Mary's lips, 'I was going anyway.' Her eyes signalled a message to Alison. 'I'll be glad to leave here—now.'

Good for you! Alison's silent nod beamed the message back. The next minute came the thought, Now it will be my turn to get my notice of dismissal. I wouldn't mind going, the way things are. *Liar, you can't bear the thought of being away from Craig, even now.* She thrust away the inner voice. But someone has to be here to attend to the housework and take care of the kids. *She* will be too busy running after Craig to even think of ordinary things like washing clothes and changing beds and keeping the cookie jars filled.

'You too, Alison,' came the imperious tones. 'There's no need for you to stay either.'

'No! Alison stays!' Craig was standing in the open doorway. 'Get it?' His tone, very quiet, very definite, brooked no argument. 'Alison's pretty important around here! She came to our rescue when Mum copped the fall off her farm bike. With the kids and all we couldn't have coped. We can't get along without her.'

Heartsick and miserable, Alison looked from Craig to Jo.

'Oh!' Jo stared blankly back at him. Her eyes narrowed as her gaze moved to Alison. 'You're the housekeeper here, then?' she asked uncertainly. Plainly, Alison thought wryly, she had been promoted in status. Could it be something in Craig's tone that was making Jo suddenly aware of the copper-haired girl in shabby jeans?

'Sort of.' Hurt and anger mingled in the glance she sent Craig. 'Girl Friday, dogsbody, land-girl, whatever——'

'Don't listen to her,' Craig cut in, 'she's my right-hand man.'

But not your woman.

She wrenched her mind back to Frances' incredulous tones. 'Do without Alison? I couldn't possibly. I always think of her as my little piece of greenstone. It's one of my Maori proverbs,' she went on to explain. 'I put it under the heading of Quality, not Quantity. *"He iti ra, he iti mapihi pounamu."* I may be small, but I am an ornament of greenstone. Frankly, I just don't know how I'm going to get along without her when she goes.' At the expression of unguarded delight that crossed Jo's face Frances added hastily, 'But that won't be for quite a while yet. It will be another month at least before I'll be able to manage on my own.'

'But I'm here,' persisted Jo.

'It's Alison I want,' Frances said stubbornly. 'She's used to me and my funny ways.' Alison realised that the older woman was kindly avoiding the truth, that as a help in the house looking after children and a semi-invalid Jo wouldn't register. 'You will stay on, won't you, Alison?'

'Of course.' Fool! You know you're grasping the opportunity that allows you to remain here in Craig's home, even knowing that he belongs to another girl. She despised herself, yet seemed powerless to tear herself away. She knew that even had Frances not been incapacitated her feelings would have been the same.

She brought her mind back to Craig's decisive tones. 'You too, Mary, you're welcome to stay for as long as you want to.'

Mary shook her head, the long dark hair falling around her face. 'Thanks a lot, Craig, but I've promised the Vasano-vichs I'd move over there for a visit just as soon as I wasn't needed here any longer. So if it's all the same to you——?'

His gaze was deep and intent. 'If that's the way you want it?'

'It is, truly. But I'll keep in touch, and I can still give you a hand with the books.'

'Thanks, Mary, but it's okay, I can manage.'

'Well then,' she leaped lightly to the floor, 'I'll go and pack my gear.' To Alison Mary didn't appear in the least put out. It was almost as if she welcomed an excuse to leave the homestead. Who could blame her now that Jo was taking over everything in her imperious manner?

'No need to take off in a hurry,' Craig told her. Then taking in her smiling gesture of denial, 'But if you insist on going I'll run you over there. We can throw your bike in the back of the Land Rover.'

Jo sent him a dazzling smile. 'I'll come with you, just for the ride.'

'There's not much room in the front.' His face still wore a bleak closed expression—but then, the gleam of hope faded as swiftly as it had come, what was a ride of a few miles to lovers who in all probability had the rest of their lives to be together?

Alison found Mary in the bedroom stuffing jeans and a denim jacket into her canvas haversack. 'It takes more than Jo to throw you,' Alison observed. 'You don't look too worried at being tossed out of here at a moment's notice.'

Mary's long eyes glimmered with secret amusement. 'Shall I tell you something? I was just wondering what excuse I could think up to get away. I've been looking forward to moving over to the Vasanovichs', but I wouldn't have gone, not while you and Frances needed me. Now it's different.'

'Different's an understatement,' Alison agreed on a sigh.

'I hate having to leave you here with her.' Mary buckled the canvas strap of her pack. 'Why don't you get going and "shoot through", as Craig would put it? Jo's always raving on about how much help she's going to be around the place, why not let her get on with it?'

Alison shook her head, the coppery curls bobbing around her face. 'I couldn't do that.'

'Why not? With Jo here——'

'Do you really think she'll do anything but please herself?'

'I guess you're right, but I'll tell you something she will do, and that is do her best to get Craig into her clutches again.'

The words brought back the ache of longing. Alison fought against it in vain. It was an effort for her to say, 'Well, I'm not risking it, not with Frances so nearly better. I'll stay as long as she wants me.' *If only it were Craig who wanted me!*

Mary's shrewd glance was altogether too perceptive. 'Are you sure you can take it?'

'Don't worry, I'll be a match for her,' but she knew that wasn't what Mary had meant.

'Well, if you're determined to stay'—Mary slipped the canvas straps over her shoulders. 'Me, I can't get away from here fast enough! But I'll come back and see you. We'll keep in touch.'

Jo strolled into the room as they were leaving. 'You're all ready now? Have you got everything?' Clearly now that she had gained her objective she could afford to be affable. 'You've got friends to go to, you said?'

'Oh yes,' Mary sent her a sleepy-eyed stare, 'I was leaving anyway.'

Alison Jo ignored. Somehow the fact of being ignored was even more humiliating than being insulted. Just a nothing person, not worth a thought. Angrily she tilted her chin once again and went out of the room while Mary went to make her farewells to Frances.

In the kitchen the twins, arriving back from school on the school bus, regarded them for a moment, then turned away to fling off sandals and cardigans.

'Say goodbye to Mary,' Alison told the children.

Two pairs of eyes gazed towards Mary in astonishment and small lips drooped. 'Are you going away?'

Mary bent to kiss each small face. ' 'Bye now, and don't worry. I'm not going far and I'll come back and see you both. You'll have Jo to look after you——'

Both children shrieked in dismay. 'Is she going to *stay* here?'

'I'm not going to do what she tells me!' yelled Patrick. 'She wouldn't let us stay up even one little minute——'

'She said only babies played with teddies!' shouted Sue in enraged tones. 'She threw away my Toby!'

'She tipped my tadpoles out of their jar,' howled Patrick. 'She said they were dirty, and they weren't! They weren't!'

'Once she hit us, *hard*——'

'Just 'cause we took a cookie from the tin without asking, and she said we could, she did, she did!'

Roused to indignation, the twins seemed bent on raking up old scores against the girl who had evidently treated them with scant regard for their helplessness.

In the uproar Mary, with a parting wave to Alison, went to seat herself in the Land Rover and Alison hustled the children away to their room. Patrick was still protesting in loud tones, 'She's not the boss of me!'

'I heard that,' Frances called, and Alison went to join the older woman in the dining room. A frown lined Frances' weathered brown forehead. 'I'm afraid they've got something to complain about with Jo. I was hoping they'd forgotten about being left in her care before, but evidently they haven't.' Her gaze moved to the window. 'There they go now. Jo's not going to enjoy her ride very much, squeezed in between the other two in the Land Rover, but I don't suppose she'll mind, so long as she's managed to get her own way. Oh dear, I do wish she'd stayed away a little longer, just until I'd got on my feet again.'

Alison, watching at the window as the vehicle swept down the winding drive, found herself wishing that Jo could have stayed away for ever. All at once anguish caught her by the throat and she stumbled blindly from the room. Fool, pull yourself together before someone guesses how you feel about him. Mary knows already, or at least suspects the truth, but she'll never tell.

'You feel things too much,' her foster-mother had often told her when Alison had been brokenhearted over the

127

death of a loved horse or a faithful farm dog, or bitterly hurt over the perfidy of a supposed friend at school. 'You take things too much to heart. You'll have to get over it, but maybe you won't. You're really just like your mother. She took things hard too.' For a moment Dot's face had softened. 'Just as long as you fall in love with the right man and he with you. Otherwise,' she shook her head, 'I don't know what you'll do.'

'Find someone else, I guess,' Alison had remarked cheerfully. She was thirteen at the time and falling in love seemed as far away as the stars of the Southern Cross pricking a kite-shape in the night sky. How simple it had all seemed then!

All at once, conscious of the heavy sweet perfume of cabbage-tree blossoms, she ran to the pottery bowl and gathering up the showers of creamy-pink flowers, flung them out of the window on to the grass below. How could she ever have imagined she liked the cloying sickly-sweet smell?

Because you couldn't run away, not when Frances had need of you—for a time. You went on with life, somehow, forcing yourself to follow the familiar pattern of household chores, trying to appear as usual heartache and all, hoping the anguish didn't show. She hadn't expected Jo to be of any real assistance in the house and indeed her help was so negligible that it scarcely counted. Not that Alison minded the extra work. In a way it kept her from thinking, most of the time.

Jo didn't get out of bed until late and by the time she had showered and made up her face lunchtime was almost on them. She insisted on sharing her midday meal with Frances, one problem solved there. The remainder of the day Jo spent either driving into the township from which she would return laden with fruit, magazines and chocolates for Frances, or flooding the older woman with needless attention. She would continue to fill flower vases and tidy up Frances' precious notes until at last Alison heard her cry in exasperation, 'I know you mean well, Jo, but for heaven's sake, will you just *leave me alone*!'

'Very well, then,' Jo had said huffily, 'if that's the way you want it. I was only trying to help.'

'I know, I know, that's just the trouble——'

The violent slamming of a door cut off the words.

So far as the twins were concerned Jo had them in a state of continual uproar. It was a different matter when Craig happened to be present, because on these occasions Jo's laughing approach and friendly attitude towards the children was in direct contrast to her usual antagonism, a fact which the children were quick to seize on and use to their own advantage.

After a stormy few days Jo gladly abandoned the twins to Alison's care. 'I can't stand kids,' she excused herself, 'especially little horrors like those two who won't do a thing they're told! Of course if I'd been in the house from the beginning it would have been a different story. As it is, you may as well keep an eye on them.' As an afterthought she added carelessly, 'It will be something for you to do!'

Something for her to do! Alison's quick temper got the better of her. 'Have you any idea,' she flared, 'of what there is to do around here?'

'Not really.' Jo's voice was bland, 'and quite frankly I don't care. I loathe farming work and everything that goes with it. I prefer to leave all those messy details to the folk who are paid to do it.'

Alison, who had been on her way to the laundry at the back of the house when Jo intercepted her, left the room before she really lost control of herself and hurled one of the 'messy details', in this case a work-stained shirt of Craig's she held in her hands, in the direction of that oh-so-superior face.

It wouldn't be for long, she reminded herself, striving for calmness. Only a few days previously the doctor, calling in to see Frances on a routine check-up, had pronounced her well on the way to recovery. 'Perhaps,' he had murmured, 'another three weeks.' One could endure anything for three weeks. Beyond that she didn't allow herself to dwell. She only knew that the mere sound of Craig's step in the porch, or the sight of his bronzed face, could stir her unbearably. Watching him ride away on a muster, she mused forlornly that only a week ago he would have been glad of her help. Now his hard impersonal gaze cut her to the heart.

One morning she was giving Banner a brush-down near the fence when she realised that Jo had intercepted Craig on his way out of the back door. The wind, blowing a gale as always up here in the hills, tossed Jo's words clearly in her direction. 'I got up specially early to see you. Seems I scarcely ever have a word in private with you these days. You're away over the hills all day and stuck in the office all night. You know something? You're a hard man to catch, and there's something I specially want to see you about. When are you going to teach me to ride? I've asked you about it so many times.'

She couldn't help overhearing both voices. Craig sounded surprised, even disbelieving. 'First I've heard of it.'

'But don't you remember all the letters I wrote you from the ship? Oh, I know you couldn't reply with me moving around all the time from port to port.'

And that's an excuse, Alison thought waspishly. He could have written ahead to one of the ports—had he wished to. The next moment hope did a nose-dive. He's proud. He would never be the first one to give in after they had parted for good. But now that Jo has made the effort the way is clear for him.

'I do want you to teach me, Craig.' Who would have believed that Jo's dominating tones could be so sweet and appealing?

'Sorry, but you'll have to wait.' Craig didn't sound unkind, merely matter-of-fact. 'I've got to go out drafting steers this morning and it's going to take me most of the day.'

Alison guessed that the refusal would do nothing for Jo's temper, always on a short fuse. But her answer when it came was honey-sweet. 'Just as you say, Craig. Seems I'll just have to wait until you get time to teach me. Unless you put off the silly old drafting? Couldn't we start today, Craig?' Alison could see Jo's hand caressing Craig's bronzed arm. She was smiling up at him beseechingly. '*Please*!'

Apparently, however, Craig was unimpressed—or more likely, Alison thought wryly, his mind was on the steers. 'Why don't you ask Alison to give you a few lessons? She's a crack rider and she'll see that you're started off in the right way. If you ask her nicely she might even let you have a go on Banner.'

Alison was aghast. Allow any novice to mount Banner! The next moment, however, she realised that her fears were groundless.

'Take lessons from her? That'll be the day!'

'Okay, it's up to you,' Craig told her, and moved away towards the stables.

Alison couldn't help a sneaky feeling of satisfaction that for once Jo wasn't having things all her own way. When she had finished grooming Banner she took the mare back to her paddock and went to wash in the bathroom. She was in the kitchen, stirring red jelly crystals in a basin, when the door was flung open.

'So there you are!' The words cut across the silent room and Alison found herself facing a girl who clearly was beside herself with anger. No doubt the fury Jo was feeling towards Craig, the disappointment and frustration, was now turned on Alison, whom for some reason she blamed for the coolness of her welcome. 'I wanted to have a word with you,' Jo's low voice throbbed with emotion. 'There are a few things we have to get straight. You might think you've been pretty clever hanging around here, getting in everyone's way. You seem to forget you're not family like the rest of us.' The emotion-charged voice rushed on before Alison could argue the point. 'So if I were you I'd make some excuse and get going. You're not wanted here and I'm warning you, *get out*! You'll get something to do. If you like,' the round eyes were empty of expression as

131

tinted glass, 'I'll fix you up with something in the domestic line myself.'

'Don't bother.' A tide of anger rose in Alison and with it the old stubbornness. Resolutely she lifted her rounded chin. She refused to be tossed out like a—a sack of dog-nuts!

'Well,' prompted the icy tones, 'I'm waiting.'

'So am I, until Frances gives me notice, tells me she doesn't want me here. Until then——'

'Oh, *you*——!' Savagely Jo spat the words out.

'Don't worry, I'll take off when Craig tells me to.'

Jo stared at her. 'Craig? So that's it?'

Alison felt cold at the pit of her stomach, but she held her ground even though she could see that Jo was almost choking with rage. For a dreadful moment she feared the other girl was about to strike her. 'You little fool! You don't really think Craig wants a kid like you hanging around here? That he *wants* you to stay? You must be out of your mind! Don't you see that he's been forced into keeping you on for a while because of the car accident? He feels under some obligation to you because of that, and he isn't one to dodge his responsibilities. You've put him in an awkward position. Now that I'm here to take over things at the house he doesn't need you any more, but he's trying to do the right thing. Surely . . .' a pitying look, 'even you can see that. Or is it that you don't want to?'

The thoughts whirled through Alison's distraught mind. Could it be true what Jo had said? The next moment she thrust the thought aside. Craig would never pretend. Whatever his personal thoughts concerning her, there was no doubt about his needing her help at his home.

Before she could make an answer Jo had hurried away. 'Don't say I didn't warn you!' she flung over her shoulder. Alison went on stirring the jelly crystals. It was a moment or two before she realised that her hands were shaking.

It was the following afternoon when once again Jo came into the kitchen where Alison sat slicing fresh beans into a basin. In that one lightning glance she realised that Jo

looked paler than usual and her eyelids were puffy, as
though she had been weeping. Jo swung herself up on a
corner of the table, swinging a sandalled foot with its gleaming pink toenails. Even without looking up Alison was
aware of the other girl's silent scrutiny. Now what? 'I've
just been down to collect the mail.' Jo began sorting out
letters addressed to herself and Frances, business letters,
farming magazines and circulars addressed to Craig. Her
tone was deceptively casual. 'You never get any mail, do
you?'

'Not yet,' Alison was choosing her words carefully, 'but
you never know your luck!'

'You don't write letters either.' And before Alison could
think up a satisfactory rejoinder, 'You're really an awfully
mysterious sort of person.' The intent gaze probed Alison's
downcast face. 'How come you never let on about yourself,
where you come from or anything?'

'Why should I?'

'It makes folks suspicious, that's all. Seems like you've no
people of your own, no boy-friend, no girl-friend even, except Mary, and I gather you only picked her up on the way
here. Frances doesn't seem to have a clue as to where you
worked before you turned up here or who your previous
employer was. Anyone would get the idea,' Alison found
she was holding her breath, 'that you were covering up,
hiding away under another name. Just a girl from nowhere!' Beneath the words Alison sensed a warning—or a
threat. The next moment she told herself that Jo couldn't
possibly know anything of her past life—*but she was doing
her utmost to find out.* 'Who but Frances,' Jo was saying,
'would take anyone into her home on trust, someone who
just walked in off the street without any credentials? I
mean, you could have been anybody——'

'Nonsense, Jo!' Neither girl had noticed that Frances
had switched off her transistor radio and now her loud
voice echoed from the adjoining room. 'Frances didn't
care about anything but being offered a helping hand by a
stranger, and that's the truth! It was a miracle to me,

Alison walking in with Mary that day. They just seemed like angels from heaven!'

'Pretty funny angels!' sneered Jo. Aloud she said crossly, 'Oh well, Frances, I suppose if you don't mind taking a risk——'

'Mind!' came the exasperated tones. 'I *love* having Alison around. I just don't know how I'm going to get along without her when she goes.'

'*When* she goes.' Only Alison caught the low meaningful words.

When Jo had left the room Alison's thoughts were in a turmoil. Happily Frances' intervention had had the effect of bypassing Jo's persistent questioning, until next time. What if in some manner she ferreted out the truth? It was unlikely that Jo would be interested enough to make inquiries, and yet . . . the niggling sense of unease remained at the back of her mind.

'You'll have to forgive Jo for the things she says,' Frances told Alison when she carried in afternoon tea. 'I can always tell when she and Craig have had another of their rows! He's got that strained look around his mouth today and she looks as though she's been crying all night!' Alison found it difficult to imagine Jo giving way to tears, and yet . . . she remembered the puffy eyelids. 'It was too bad of her to take out her bad temper on you. You won't take any notice of what she said, will you?'

'Of course not.' Alison was thinking that at least she must have convinced Craig that he had nothing to be concerned about regarding her past life, for he appeared to be satisfied with her evasive answers to his inquiries. Oh, why not face up to the truth and admit to yourself that he's simply lost interest in your affairs now that he has Jo here with him!

Thoughtfully Frances sipped her tea. 'I wonder,' she remarked thoughtfully, 'what the trouble was between Jo and Craig this time. *You*, probably.'

'Me?' Alison attempted to cover the betraying squeak with a careless laugh. 'I don't see——'

134

'Oh, he's always talking about you,' Frances stated calmly. 'He thinks you're wonderful.'

'In what . . . way?'

'Every way, according to him. He likes the way you keep house, says it seems to be no effort to you to have everything done and meals always ready on time no matter what time he happens to come home. No clutter anywhere and the children so well cared for. Outside too . . . he says when it comes to mustering and drafting you're as good as a man.'

'Oh,' Alison could feel her spirits dropping back to their usual heavy position these days, 'those sort of things.'

Frances looked surprised. 'They mean a lot to a man on his own, especially now that I've gone and developed this stupid sore leg.'

'I guess he thinks I'm handy to have around the place,' the brave words belied the pain shadowing her eyes. 'Handy' —but it was Jo with her voluptuous body and dominating personality who fascinated him.

One afternoon a strange car pulled up in the driveway and Mary strolled along the path escorted by a tall young man with dark eyes and a pleasant expression. Alison felt sure this must be Tony Vasanovich. A different Mary, this, Alison couldn't help thinking, for her friend radiated a sense of happiness and the sleepy eyes were brilliant. After a time Craig, calling back at the house, took Tony out to the paddocks to see a new foal and Jo, uninvited, hurried after them.

Mary's gaze followed Jo as she trailed alongside the two men. 'Things are just the same here, then?' She took in Alison's pale face and shadowed eyes. 'You're not over-doing it, are you, with all the extra work?'

'No, no, I'm just losing a bit of my tan. It comes of being inside so much.'

Mary was altogether too perceptive. 'No more riding with Craig these days?'

'I've got far too much to do indoors,' Alison said quickly, 'I haven't a hope of getting outside.'

'Well, at least you're sticking it out and proving a match for you-know-who.'

But not when it comes to love. Swiftly she made to change the subject. 'How about you? Are you one of the family yet?'

Mary sent her a startled glance. 'Oh, I see what you mean. It's funny,' she gazed dreamily over soaring sheep-threaded hills, 'but it seems like home to me over there, has done ever since the first moment when I walked in at the door.'

'Are you sure,' teased Alison, 'that you'd like it so much at the Vasanovichs' if Tony weren't there?'

'Tony?' Suddenly Mary was confused. A dull pink suffused her face and she played nervously with a cuff-button of her denim blouse. 'Whatever makes you think he has anything to do with it?'

Alison laughed. 'There must be some attraction, and you're always talking to me about him over the phone. Not that I blame you, he's very good-looking. Tall like you, nice manners, the sort of man you couldn't help liking.'

'He's okay.' Mary's voice was muffled and she jumped to her feet. 'I'd better have a word with Frances. She's sure to have oodles of typing ready for me by now. Isn't it lucky that all farmers seem to have an ancient typewriter kicking around the office?' She smiled reminiscently, 'Who would ever have dreamed that I'd land in New Zealand and right away start on becoming an authority of Maori proverbs?' She tossed the long dark hair back from her shoulders. 'I do miss Frances and her proverbs. She could always produce one to fit the occasion.' She giggled. 'D'you remember her telling Jo that you were her "little bit of greenstone"? I don't think Jo appreciated it very much. Come to that, I don't imagine Jo likes anything here very much, except Craig, of course. I must fly——'

Mary rang through on the following day, her tone so warm and alive with happiness that Alison found herself saying wistfully, 'You still seem to be enjoying yourself over there.'

'Oh, I am! I am!'

The two chatted for a time, making arrangements for Alison to visit Mary on the following evening, then Mary broke off—'Wait a minute, Nick's here beside me. He wants to have a word with you, but only, and I quote, if you want to speak to him.'

'Of course I want to speak to him.' Poor Nick, in her troubled state of mind she had all but forgotten him.

'Alison! Can you forgive me for what happened the other night?' She caught the note of distress in the low tones. 'I've been wanting to tell you, to come over and make it right with you, but it didn't work out.' She recalled Craig's warning to Nick that he was to keep away from her. 'I tried to get through to you on the phone, but had no luck——' So he had been unfortunate enough to have had his call answered by Craig. 'But that doesn't mean to say I haven't been worried stiff about you. Mary tells me you're all right, but I can't help wondering——'

'Of course I'm all right. I'm fine, no harm done. How about you?'

'Oh, all I copped from the smash was a stiff ankle and the odd bruise. Nothing bad enough to keep me from entering in the rodeo events next month.'

'And your car?'

'Tony's car, you mean. It's still in the garage in town. Tony's not being very co-operative about that. He tells me I've got to pay the repair bill even if it takes me the rest of my life to settle it. I wouldn't put it past him,' he confided morosely, 'to add interest on the money as well. No pity, no brotherly love ...'

Alison laughed. 'Fair enough.'

'Oh, forget old Tony. It's you I'm interested in. It seems an age since—Look,' all at once he was excited, 'Mary tells me you're coming over here tomorrow night.' Urgency laced the boyish tones. 'You will make it? Promise?'

'I'll come.'

'That's all I wanted to know. You've made my day. 'Bye.'

She replaced the receiver and swung around to meet

137

Craig's grave, intent gaze. 'Who was that on the blower?'

She hesitated for barely a second. He would scarcely be interested in young Nick, not now, so why trouble with explanations? 'That was Mary on the phone. She rings me most days. She's invited me to go over there to see her tomorrow evening.'

'Mighty! It'll get you out of the house for a bit. A good idea.'

A good idea for whom? For him and Jo, to enable them to make up their recent disagreement in privacy?

He said, 'I'll run you over there and pick you up later.'

'But there's no need,' she protested. 'I've got the Mini. I've scarcely used it for ages and the battery ...' the words died into silence beneath his brooding stare.

'I'll take you.' The tense lines around his mouth relaxed a little. 'It's a date, then?'

'I guess.' A date for him and Jo? An opportunity for them to be alone together? The thought came to torture her that for a few hours at least Craig wouldn't be forced to carry on his love affair under the eyes of a silly romantic girl who had read into his light caresses a depth of feeling he had never intended. She felt the prick of tears behind her eyelashes and was glad that Frances, calling to him at that moment, summoned him away.

That evening at dinner Jo's strong accents dominated the conversation. Could it be Craig's withdrawn manner, Alison wondered, that was causing the other girl to run on like this, as though she couldn't bear silence? Jo was describing in some detail her travels overseas, the varied exotic foods she had sampled during her short stay in distant lands. Always the anecdotes would conclude with a light and laughing reference to the many men she had met during her travels, the attentions lavished upon her by influential friends and the escorts who had competed for the pleasure of taking her dining and dancing.

Even in the midst of heartache Alison was aware of a note of over-excitement running through the monologue. Who was Jo trying to impress? Frances, seated on a couch nearby, injured leg propped up on a stool and tea-tray balanced on her ample lap, appeared suitably awed by the mention of well-known names, but Craig said little and the discourse appeared to be passing him by. There must indeed have been a bitter quarrel between these two, but they would make it up again. Hadn't Frances told her that they always had in the past?

As she passed around mugs of steaming coffee Alison was only half aware of Jo's superior tones. 'Of course everyone knows that travel broadens the mind, gives one a wider outlook. I've been lucky, I suppose, everyone can't get around the world as I did. Take Alison now——' why must Jo speak of her as though she weren't in the room? The slightly protruding eyes with their suspicious expression were fixed on Alison's downcast face. 'Bet you've never been far from your own little corner of the world, wherever that is. Where do you come from, anyway?'

Alison, pouring coffee into a pottery beaker, pulled herself together. 'Me? Oh, just down country a bit——' Unfortunately she couldn't control the trembling of her hands and coffee spilled over on to the cloth. If only no one had noticed. Apparently, however, someone had, for Jo's avid tone quickened. 'You sound awfully vague about it.' A wicked light like a tiny bulb burned in the blue eyes.

'It's such a small place, scarcely on the map even. You would never have heard of it.'

'Try me,' challenged Jo. 'I've been over most parts of the country one time or another.'

Alison didn't answer and Jo's glance moved from Alison's flushed cheeks to Craig's closed face. 'I suppose Alison has always worked with sheep and cattle,' somehow she contrived to make the activities seem distasteful, 'wherever she came from? Come on now, Alison, don't be so secretive —where was it?'

'Nowhere important.' Why was she such a colossal fool when it came to lies and deception? Why couldn't she have made mention of a name previously, any name, and thus avoided this interrogation which she felt sure was being staged with a deliberate attempt at planting suspicions in Craig's mind.

He was stowing away the makings, tobacco and flimsy papers, in the pocket of his cotton shirt. 'It wouldn't ring a bell with you, Jo. Anyway,' he drawled, 'it's not where she comes from that matters. It's what she does that counts around here.'

Jo shot Alison a glance of pure hatred. 'I wouldn't know, never having been domestic.'

Alison had never seen Craig's eyes look so hard. He rose to his feet, pushing back his chair. 'If you'll excuse me, folks, I've got to get cracking.'

CHAPTER NINE

ALISON had bathed the twins and put them to bed before she showered and changed into an ankle-length dress of flower-patterned cotton. She was moving down the hall when Craig joined her. 'All ready?'

'Ready and waiting, sir!' He paused, taking in her sweet young face with its wistful expression. Did she imagine a softening of the harsh lines of his face? The next moment Jo opened her bedroom door, her resentful tones shattering the moment of silence. 'I don't see why you have to go out tonight, Craig. Surely Alison's got her own car in the garage?'

'She doesn't know the way,' he explained briefly. 'Besides, I've got to make sure she gets home safely.'

Alison turned away with a forlorn droop of her shoulders. Of course . . . his right-hand man.

Out in the purple dusk car-lights beamed down the winding track as they swept down to the gates. Alison jumped out of the car to open and close them, then they were out on the main highway. A single star glittered low in the darkening sky and cicadas piped their endless summer song from the sombre bush at the roadside.

'This is new territory to you, isn't it?'

'That's right.' How distant was his voice, as though she were a stranger to whom he was giving a lift. To break the strained silence she heard herself chattering wildly. 'I— haven't been out anywhere lately. I've been sticking close to home——' did that sound like a complaint? 'With one thing and another.' Heavens, now he might imagine that she was criticising Jo for the other girl's lack of co-operation.

His thoughtful glance underlined her suspicions. 'You've been working flat-stick lately. Not much fun, but it won't be for long now.'

'No.' Anguish like a dark cloud enveloped her spirit. If only he weren't so devastatingly attractive! If only she had insisted on driving her own car tonight.

The well-shaped hand on the wheel was firm and he drove swiftly and competently. Presently he began to speak of nothing things, farming procedures, local history, the names of the hills rising in the distance. The miles flew by and before long they were turning off the main road and taking a winding drive that led towards a comfortable-looking, red-roofed house half hidden amongst tall native trees.

He let her out at the entrance to the house. 'What time shall I pick you up? Eleven, twelve? Just say the word.'

Flustered, she said, 'Eleven will do.'

'Right. See you.' He swung around in the driveway and she ran up the front steps, the long folds of her dress falling around her ankles. Before she could put a finger to the door chimes Mary had opened the door and was drawing her inside. 'Lovely to see you!'

'You too!' They strolled down the long hall with its shelves of trailing plants.

Mary said, 'How's everything over at Craig's place? Jo still throwing her weight about?'

'You know Jo.'

'And Frances, how is she?'

'Oh, she's ever so much better. She——' Alison's words were drowned in a gale of voices as the two girls entered the big old-fashioned lounge room. Nick's parents greeted her warmly, as did Grandmother Vasanovich. Around her pressed a group of tall muscular men, all with dark hair and eyes, all welcoming her at once in their loud voices. Someone asked her to sit down on a couch, then the babel of voices broke out again, inquiring after her health. Was she O.K. after the accident? Young Nick, his older brothers assured her, would never get away with that sort of thing again, especially with her in the car, they could promise her that! A young man who appeared to be only slightly older than Nick told her his name was Ivan and offered her wine. Presently she became aware that Nick had squeezed into the seat beside her. 'Gee, I'm sorry about the smash——' He did indeed look crushed, Alison thought, and no wonder, with the constant reprimands of his brothers. 'Forget about it,' she smiled, and turned her attention to Tony, standing nearby. 'How badly was the car damaged?'

'It wasn't too extensive after all.' He had an attractive voice, she mused, quiet, well-spoken in contrast to the wild exuberance of his brothers. 'Not that it mattered so long as you and Nick haven't any serious injuries.'

'Only his pride,' put in the mischievous-eyed Ivan. 'Do you know what he said about you?' She realised Nick was frantically trying to signal his brother to silence, to no avail. 'He told us you were the most fantastic girl he'd ever met in his life! He said he'd never met anyone like you and then he'd gone and blued his chances! He was feeling so low about it he was thinking about shooting himself, but when we offered to do it for him he seemed to change his mind all of a sudden.'

In the guffaws of laughter Nick edged nearer to Alison. 'You really mean that, about it being all right now? You don't hold it against me?'

Looking down at his downcast young face, she felt a prick of compassion. 'Of course I don't.'

Nick's expression cleared. 'Tremendous! I can't believe it! I was coming over to tell you I was sorry about it all, ask you to let me off the hook——'

'Why didn't you?'

Nick looked acutely embarrassed and it was Ivan, listening unashamedly to the conversation, who answered. 'He's scared stiff of your boss, that's why! He says the guy's nuts about you and he'd eat him alive if he as much set a foot in the place.'

Nuts about you! If only it were so!

'It's true, isn't it?'

She became ware of Nick's anxious gaze. Swiftly she gathered together her wildly-flying thoughts.

'What's true? That Craig was mad about the crash? He

was rather,' her lips curved in a sad little smile, 'but only because he seems to have an idea you're a menace on the road——'

'Not any more! You've got to believe me——'

'You're not going to trust *his* word,' came Ivan's jeering voice. 'You just don't know him like we do.'

Nick wasn't listening. 'But it was *you* he was so het up about.'

She shook her head. 'Craig would have been concerned about anyone in the car that night.' How weak the statement sounded! But the alternative was so fantastic, so utterly improbable it didn't bear thinking about.

Oddly, Nick persisted in the ridiculous supposition. 'You can't tell me that guy's concern was for any old body. It was the way he looked——'

'Forget him.' The talk about Craig was making her embarrassed and stupidly happy, raising hopes that had no possibility of fulfilment. All that, she reminded herself, was before Jo's arrival at the house.

It seemed no time at all before she was urged into the old-fashioned kitchen where a huge spread was laid out on the long kauri table. 'This isn't just supper?' Alison whispered to Mary, looking in surprise at the assortment of foods.

'They were so pleased about you coming tonight,' Mary whispered back. 'They're trying to make up to you for what happened, you know?'

'Nice of them.' But she found herself wishing that the family could have expressed their good wishes in some other way. At the house she tried to disguise the fact that she had little appetite. How could she pretend beneath these watching eyes?

At last, however, the plates were emptied, coffee cups taken away and Mary drew her away to the privacy of her own room.

'All that supper!' groaned Alison. 'I can scarcely move.'

'I know, but they meant it kindly.'

'I like your room.' Alison was taking in the spacious bedroom with its gleaming floors of polished wood and scattered fluffy sheepskin rugs, the plain old chest of drawers and long picture windows. She dropped down on the neatly made bed with its yellow spread. 'I've brought you the latest instalment of Frances' proverbs. Hope you're not too busy here to type it out for her.'

'No, no, I'll do it.' Absently Mary took the clipped folder Alison extended towards her. She said with studied carelessness, 'What do you think of Tony?'

'The quiet one? I like him a lot.'. Alison reflected that Tony would be an ideal mate for Mary. Tall and dark with a nice manner, confident yet not too confident and of just the right age. She knew that Craig had taken a liking to him too and somehow that was what counted. Aloud she murmured, 'You told me about him the first time you came to his home. He's the clever one who's a fully fledged barrister.'

'That's him, that's Tony. I thought you'd like him. Look,' she was speaking rapidly, nervously, in a most un-Marylike manner, 'he gave me this.' She lifted the tiny translucent heart carved from amber swinging from a leather thong around her neck.

Alison eyed the smooth little shape.

'It's kauri gum! Is it made from gum dug up around here?'

'Is it ever! It's quite old, actually. Tony's grandfather carved it out of gum he dug up in the district when he first arrived here from Yugoslavia. Seems he made some sort of living from the gumfields, living in a tent until he could afford to build a house. They say there's very little of the gum about the district, now that the kauri trees have mostly been cut down or burned.' She seemed to be running on. 'Tony wanted to give me something else,' restlessly she fingered the small heart shape. 'A ring, his grandmother's engagement ring, but I couldn't take it.' A frown etched itself along her smooth forehead and there was a worried note in her voice, 'I just couldn't! I mean, how could he love me—*really* love me, so soon?'

145

'It's happened before.' There was no need to ask if Mary loved him, Alison thought. It was there for anyone to read in the low unsteady voice, the words that were tumbling from her lips in an obvious attempt to ease her own uncertainty of mind.

'Was it because of the ring?' Alison queried gently. 'Didn't the family approve of your having it?'

Mary stared back at her. 'Oh no, nothing like that. They wanted me to have it. That was the trouble.'

Alison looked bewildered. 'I don't get it. If the family are happy about the idea and so are you and Tony——'

'The family! The family!' Suddenly Mary's usually composed tones were rising out of control. 'They're so close, they do everything, but *everything*, together. Grandmother Vasanovich's word is law, you wouldn't believe it! How do I know,' Mary cried passionately, 'he really loves me, wants me *himself* and not just to please his people. Don't you see what I mean? Here they all are, living in this practically womanless community, and one day in I walk with all the right qualifications. Mama Vasanovich is a darling, I'm fond of her, but she tells me I'd make a perfect wife for one of her sons. She probably wouldn't care which one. How do I know he loves me for myself?'

'But hasn't he told you——'

'Of course he has, lots of times, but I don't know whether I can believe him. I keep remembering that he spent years and years studying for the law and then tossed it all away—and why? Simply because the family had taken over a bigger property and could do with his office training as well as his help on the land. Doesn't that go to show that his family come first and his own feelings way behind?'

Alison hesitated. 'Problems, problems. Well,' she said with conviction, 'I think you should believe him.'

You think, jeered a small inner voice from somewhere deep in her mind. Who are you to hand out advice to another girl? Didn't Craig tell you that he loved you? Did you believe him? That was different. So *you* say. The small niggling voice refused to be silenced.

146

Craig arrived at the house promptly at eleven o'clock and despite pressing invitations from the Vasanovich family to stay, even if only just long enough to drink a glass of wine with them, he insisted on leaving at once. Because of Jo waiting at home, Alison wondered bleakly, getting into the car. As they moved away she put on her gayest smile and waved to the group gathered together on the long verandah.

The blue-blackness of the night sky was pricked by scintillating stars and a soft wind caressed her face. She was reminded of one of Frances' expressions, 'the soft west wind of love.' Love . . . She stole a glance towards the stern masculine profile at her side.

She must be dreaming. His strained expression, the set line of his jaw, scarcely indicated a man who was happily reunited with his lost love, but then there had been a quarrel between him and Jo. Tonight he made no effort to throw an arm about her shoulders. Why should he bother with make-believe when he had the reality at hand? Could it be that his hard angry look had something to do with herself? Maybe he was remembering those brief moments of tenderness between them, asking himself how best to put an end to any romantic feelings she might happen to have on his account. With a shame-making feeling of humiliation she remembered his mention of that expressive face of hers.

'Had a good time tonight?' He didn't lift his gaze from the road ahead.

'Oh yes,' she roused herself to answer him, 'it was super meeting them all. Mary seems to have really settled in over there——'

His voice was steel. 'You didn't go making any arrangements with young Nick to see him again?'

'No, no, I didn't!' Too late she thought up a better rejoinder. 'What is it to you if I did?' In the darkness her lips quirked in a wry smile. And Nick had actually got the idea that this man, this dark angry man seated beside her, had been crazy about her!

He drove in silence and the miles fell away on the long straight road where there seemed nothing in the world but the dark bush at either side of the highway and the beam of the headlamps illuminating a fragment of roadway ahead. Lost in her thoughts, she was surprised when suddenly he braked to a stop, pulling in at the side of the lonely, bush-fringed road.

'What's wrong?' she jerked herself upright. 'Not trouble?'

He turned to face her, the line of his jaw set in the dim light of the dashboard. 'Big trouble—no, not the car,' as her eyes widened in alarm.

'Then what——' For no reason at all she felt the heavy thud-thud of her heart.

'Alison, there's something we've got to get straightened out——'

'You don't have to tell me,' she was in a flurry of pain. A sick sense of humiliation made her rush on. 'It's O.K., you know.'

She was aware of his startled look. 'What do you mean?'

Idiot! By forcing the subject she had got herself into an embarrassing position, but she had no course but to follow it through. 'Oh, nothing, just about you and Jo——'

His voice was dangerously quiet. 'What about it?'

'Oh, you know what I mean.' Confusion carried off whatever sense she had left. 'Frances told me all about you and her.'

'You don't know.' His voice was very low.

'Enough.' She scarcely knew what she was saying. 'You don't have to spell it out.' She only knew she must cling to whatever remnants of pride she had left. 'I understand.'

'Damn it all, you don't!'

Before she realised his intention his arms were around her and he had gathered her close, close. The old betraying sense of wild excitement took over.

'It's you I love, Alison.' His lips sought hers in a kiss that sent her pulses leaping wildly in response.

At last, shaken and trembling, she drew away. Her heart

was thudding madly. 'Don't!' she whispered brokenly. Madness to believe his protestations of love with Jo waiting for him at home. Once again his dark good looks and masculine magnetism had betrayed her into forgetting all the important things, the things that mattered, like Jo's assured position in his home, her planing of renovations to the house where she would soon be mistress.

'You don't expect me to believe you?' Her voice had a high wild note, but evidently the message got through because his arms fell away from her. 'Why shouldn't you believe me?'

'You ask me why, with Jo——'

'Forget Jo!' he said roughly, and made a move towards her, but she was on her guard now against the betraying magic of his touch.

'Sorry, but I can't, not even to please you!'

Anger flared in his tone. 'Look, you might give me a chance to explain.'

'You might have told me about Jo,' she said very low, 'before I made a fool of myself. I'll go,' she told him nervously, unhappily, 'just as soon as——'

'You won't, you know! You'll stay until I can get you to understand a few things I can't seem to get through to you.'

'It's no use——'

'Right!' His low angry tone cut her to the heart. 'I've told you how I feel. If you choose to think differently, if that's what you want to believe——' Savagely he thrust a hand towards the starter and they shot forward.

What she wanted. Oh, Craig, if you only knew!

She huddled in a corner of the seat as far away from him as possible. Craig never drove in this manner, recklessly and wildly. She had really upset him this time, but it was no more than he deserved. Imagine thinking he could make a pretence of loving her while all the time he and Jo were planning their future life together! Well, she had made it plain to him that she wouldn't play his game and there was no doubt he was angry, surprised too. But what could he expect her to do in such circumstances? Funny—moisture stung her eyes as they swept on in the darkness—you would imagine that having done the right thing you would feel better about it, that it would be a load off your mind, yet she felt no such reaction, only a terrible anguish that seemed to be tearing her apart.

For a crazy moment she was tempted to take him on any terms, but almost immediately the thought died. Anyway, he was no longer interested in her, you could tell that from his stormy dark face, the hard set of his jaw. She swallowed and bit her lip to stop the trembling. If only Jo hadn't come to spoil everything she might have had a chance of happiness. Craig's 'It's you I love' might have been true.

The uneasy silence seemed to her to last for ever, but at last they were turning in at the homestead gates. Alison wrenched herself from unhappy musing, realising that although the rest of the house was in darkness, lights streamed from the windows of the room where the twins were sleeping. As Craig braked to a stop at the garage, she let herself out and hurried away. 'I'd better see what's wrong with the kids.'

He made no answer and she fled into the house. In the lighted room two red and tear-stained faces looked up at her, then the twins were hurling themselves towards her.

'She wouldn't read us a story!'

'She wouldn't let us have the light on. She took away my lamp.' Patrick was terrified of the darkness and Alison had made a special trip to the township to get him a tiny light with a low-powered bulb. 'She says she's going to throw it away in the gully tomorrow,' howled Patrick. 'She called me a baby to want it.'

'She wouldn't let us get up to get a drink of water!' Sue added her complaint.

The two indignant voices were shouting in unison, 'But we got a drink of water when she went out for a walk with Uncle Craig!'

'Yea, and two biscuits.' Triumphantly Patrick concluded

150

the triumphant recital. 'An' we got back into bed and she didn't know.'

'Well, you'll be all right now. Look, here's your little light.' Alison picked it up from beneath the bed and fitted in the plug, then switched off the bright centre light. When she returned to seat herself on the bed the little girl's freckled arms went around Alison's neck. 'We love you, Alison.'

Patrick hurled himself towards her and she was half-smothered in a bear-hug. 'You won't ever leave us again, will you, 'cause we love you and we hate you going away!'

'We won't let you!' Another embrace from Sue.

Something, some sense of being watched, made her look up to meet Craig's brooding gaze. How strange he looked, so stern and forbidding. Yet when he spoke his voice was gentle. 'That'll do, you two. Let Alison get some sleep.'

She straightened the top sheets, rolled into balls, and pulled the bedclothes over the children. 'Go to sleep now. See you in the morning.'

'See you in the morning,' echoed two sleepy voices.

Leaving the dim light burning, Alison turned away, aware all the time of Craig standing in the doorway. What was he waiting for, and where was Jo?

'Alison——' She avoided his gaze. There was one thing she must remember, and that was not to let herself be alone with him. Resolutions were fine in their way, but she knew that he had only to hold her in his arms once again and it would be harder than ever to make herself remember the important things, like Jo.

''Night, Craig.' She hurried past him and fled up the passage. In the turmoil of her heart she was vaguely aware of the sound of someone sobbing, a sound that came from Jo's room. So the walk she and Craig had taken tonight hadn't mended their recent quarrel? Difficult to imagine Jo crying into her pillow. Anger, yes, retaliation too, but tears ...

Lying in bed a little later, she told herself she had done the right thing in refusing to be led into a midnight talk

151

alone with Craig. Only if it was the right thing, why did it hurt so much?

As the days crept by Alison found herself living from day to day, if you could call it living. Really it was existing, watching for Craig, listening for the deep tones of his voice as in the evenings he spent the time at the telephone, deep in discussions with stock agents, veterinary surgeons and carriers. At these times Jo would glance impatiently at the clock, wriggling in her chair and at last, with an angry expression, go to her room. To Alison it seemed a strange courtship between Jo and Craig, but then, she reminded herself, there were countless couples who appeared to thrive on disagreements and reunions. If Craig was happy ... certainly he showed little evidence of contentment. Had the deep lines always etched themselves down his lean cheeks, his face been set so grimly? Could be the trouble lay in herself, a third party in his home, but he had refused to let her go and she knew she was bound by the ties of love that held her here until Frances was able to look after the household herself. By that time Jo and Craig might have set a wedding date. The thought was never far from her mind.

It was a relief to escape occasionally from the house, to jump into the Mini and drive over to visit Mary—for at the Vasanovich home her welcome was always warm and uncomplicated.

'Here she is! She's here!' Mama Vasanovich would cry as the little car paused in the driveway. 'Mary! Where are you? Alison's come to see you!' By the time Alison was inside all the family would be there to welcome her, all talking at once telling her the latest news of family and farm doings. Always there would be Nick hurrying towards her, his face glowing as if a lantern had been lighted behind the dark eyes, the words spilling excitedly from his lips in the pleasure of seeing her once again.

Today, however, Mary appeared to be acting strangely, waving an arm in the air and sending silent messages over Alison's head to others in the room.

152

'We'll have to tell her,' Mary cried at last, 'she's never going to notice!' Only then did Alison realise that on Mary's third finger gleamed an antique ring set with rubies and pearls.

'Mary! I didn't notice!' Her own heartache must have blinded her to the ring that had been repeatedly pushed beneath her gaze. Everyone talked and laughed at once. Tony came out of his office and stood at Mary's side, proud and happy and smiling, accepting Alison's congratulations. Papa Vasanovich opened a bottle of wine, the precious vintage reserved for special family occasions and toasts were drunk to the newly-engaged couple.

It was only after a huge lunch had been eaten and cleared away that the two girls escaped to the privacy of Mary's room.

'I'm glad for you,' Alison told her friend, 'It's wonderful that things worked out right after all.' Her eyes glimmered with a teasing light. 'I knew you loved Tony——'

'All the time,' Mary's serious face glowed with a deep inner radiance, 'more than anyone in the whole world! What I was worried about was, did he love me?'

'Oh yes, the family——'

'But it wasn't at all like I thought. Tony did give up his training for law, but it was his own idea and he had plenty of family opposition to contend with.'

'He told you about it?'

Mary shook her head, her gaze fixed on the jewelled ring encircling her finger.

'It was Mama who put everything right for me. She told me that Tony had never wanted to be a lawyer or to live or work in the city. All he had ever wanted to do, right from childhood, was to work on the land with his father and brothers. It was his parents who set their heart on his following a career. It seems he was very clever at school and they followed the principal's advice at the college and insisted on his having training for law. To please them he stuck it out, he even worked at it for a time, but the family took over a bigger holding and there was need of his trained mind to keep an eye on the business side of things, need of another man too on the farm, he saw his chance to get back to the work he loves. Grandmother Vasanovich had lots of arguments with him about it, but he held out for the sort of life he wanted—and got it.' She smiled her secret smile. 'And got me as well.' For a moment her face grew serious. 'If only things could have worked out for you too!'

'Your wedding,' Alison cut in quickly, 'when is it to be? You'll have to give me time to get something ready to wear.'

Mary's sleepy eyes saw entirely too much and an understanding heart supplied the rest.

'We haven't decided yet. Things are just the same, then, with Jo and Craig?'

Alison looked away. 'They've known each other ... for a long time.'

'Too long, maybe. Craig doesn't strike me as a man who's madly in love—at least, not with Jo. There's nothing more dead than a burned-out love affair, one that's really finished. Jo's wasting her time trying to revive it.'

Alison didn't know that her eyes were lighted with a wild gleam of hope. 'Do you really think so?'

'Ask yourself. Especially as everything's different now.'

But Alison wasn't listening. The surge of hope had died away leaving her with the old sick feeling of misery, the hopeless longing. Wishful thinking will get you nowhere. She jerked her thoughts away from thoughts of Craig and said, 'Frances wanted me to give you the last chapter of her proverbs book to type.' She took from her suede bag the folded sheets of handwriting. 'She just made it in time. She'll be on her feet pretty soon with lots to do——'

'And you'll be moving on?'

'Don't worry, I'll keep in touch.' Alison raised a tremulous face, 'Wherever I am I'll be back for your wedding.'

They went on to discuss details of the forthcoming wedding and Nick's car that was due to arrive on the follwing day.

'He's determined to behave himself from now on,' Mary told her. 'Craig's laying it on the line that he wasn't to come near you at his home really hit him hard. He can't wait to prove what a reformed character he is.'

Alison laughed, 'Poor Nick!' but she wasn't really concerned.

The next morning began as usual. She followed the usual routine into which she had fallen since Jo's arrival. First there were breakfasts to be attended to, then the usual household chores and Frances to be comfortably settled for the day. After that came the part of the day she most looked forward to, when she went up the slope to the paddock not far from the house, saddled Banner, then went flying over the gates and up and down grassy slopes encircled with the tracks made by a myriads sheep. Black steers grazing on the hills scattered madly at the approach of the small copper-headed figure mounted on the graceful white mare and sheep milled wildly ahead of the flying hoofs.

There were times when she would catch a glimpse of Craig as he repaired a boundary fence or mustered sheep on the hills, but although every nerve in her body strained towards him she would guide Banner in the opposite direction. No sense in multiplying the memories—and the anguish.

Today as she emerged from a bush track through a gully she caught sight of Craig a short distance away. He was mounted on Pax, one of the stock horses, and gestured for Alison to join him, but she shook her head and went on, urging Banner to a fast canter.

A shout made her glance back over her shoulder to find Craig in pursuit. Well, if he wanted a race he should have it! She leaned forward and encouraged Banner to a faster pace. Ahead loomed a steep slope, but the mare didn't hesitate. Now Alison could hear behind her the thud-thud of galloping hoofs on the turf—but he hadn't caught up with her yet. Half way down the incline rose a seven-barred fence. She heard his warning call but took no notice, clinging with her knees to the white flanks. The fence was directly ahead. 'Come on Banner, you can do it!' The mare gathered herself together spread out and sailed effortlessly over the barbed wires running across the hillside. Another minute and Craig's horse landed on the ground directly behind her, then he was riding level grasping her rein. At last flushed and laughing with exhilaration, she drew Banner to a halt.

'You didn't tell me,' surprise and delight mingled in his tone, 'you were a top show-jumper!'

Caught in the pleasure of the moment, she forgot everything else and turned a smiling face towards him. 'You didn't ask me!'

'That's done it!' He turned towards her as the horses paced surefootedly down the steep incline. Suddenly his eyes were ablaze with excitement, almost ... elation. Surely what she had done didn't warrant such a look! 'I've got news for you! How would you like to go with me to an A. & P. show they're putting on at the showgrounds on Saturday? Enter Banner in one of the hack events?'

'Fabulous!' Her face was alight with pleasure. 'Oh, *could* we?'

'Why not? You get Banner ready for showing and I'll see to everything else. We could put the mare in the truck.' Enthusiasm rang in his tone. 'We'll enter Banner in the Champion Hunter event and see how she does. You'll know what to do, you've done it all before.'

'Lots of times.' Today she couldn't lie to him. 'I brought my saddle with me.'

'Tremendous! The way I look at it, it's a chance to find out what she's capable of.' Craig glanced towards her as the horses moved side by side in the bright hot sunshine. 'I've only had Banner for a short while and I haven't a clue as to how she performs in the show ring. For all I know the hurdy-gurdy music might scare her stiff or the fluttering of the flags around the arena put her off. I told you before, the mare doesn't belong to me.'

'You did say something about it.' Alison daren't raise her glance for fear he would read the truth in her eyes.

'So I'd be interested to find out her capabilities in the ring. This is your chance, Alison, yours and Banner's. Win the Champion Hunter event and you'll collect a silver cup and be in the money to the tune of seventy odd dollars. What more could you want?'

What more? The wild surge of excitement ebbed, leaving only the ache of longing. 'You seem to have an awful lot of faith in Banner?'

'In *you*, Alison.' How deep and vibrant was his tone, almost ... caressing. Had she not been aware of the relationship between him and Jo she could almost have imagined ... He said softly, 'Didn't I ever tell you?'

A little more of this, she thought in panic, his warm expression, the tenderness in his tone, and she would be lost. With an effort she forced herself back to sanity. 'You're wrong, you know. Banner is a horse in a million, the sort you only come across once or twice in a lifetime. I just let her have her head.' Belatedly she realised she was speaking of the mare as though she had known her for a long time. She added quickly, 'If you feel like that about her why don't you ride her yourself at the show?'

'Aha——!' Craig's eyes were dancing with a teasing light and all at once a terrible fear shot through her. He couldn't possibly have discovered the truth about Banner and her previous owner, he couldn't! She found she was holding her breath.

'It's just,' he was saying 'that Banner has been used to being ridden by a girl. Chances are she mightn't perform as usual if I took her around the show ring. Like I said, I want to get a true picture of what she can do.'

'I see.' Somewhere deep inside her a tightly coiled spring seemed to unwind. So he didn't know. It was only her own sense of guilt that had lent significance to his words. Reassured, she looked up into his face and felt confusion, wild and sweet, sweep through her. 'Come on, race you to the big tree down there!' She urged Banner forward and the two mounts took off along the straight and galloping side by side, reached the tree at the same moment. As she and Craig pulled in Alison caught sight of the school bus moving along the road far below. 'Golly, I've got to get back. Frances will be wanting her afternoon tea and the twins——' The words trailed away as she turned her mount.

'Don't forget—day after tomorrow's Show Day!' Craig called after her.

'I won't! Goodbye!' She pressed her heels to Banner's sides and was away, escaping from the temptation of falling deeper in love with a man who wasn't for her. She risked a swift backward glance. He sat motionless, looking after her. Was he waiting to see her safely over the barbed wires of a sheep-fence looming ahead? There was no need for anxiety on her behalf. Hadn't she and her mare taken countless more difficult jumps at shows and local hunts? The mare performed faultlessly, clearing the top wire easily to land safely on the green grass at the opposite side. As Banner moved on Alison allowed herself one more backward glance. He was still looking towards her. She saw him raise his hand in a salute. Just ordinary politeness, of course, he would have done the same for any girl rider who had safely negotiated a difficult jump.

Craig was home early for dinner that evening and it was he who brought up the subject of the forthcoming A. & P. Show to be held in the showgrounds of a neighbouring township at the weekend.

'An A. & P. Show! Super!' Jo's excited voice cut across the laconic tones. 'I haven't been to one in years. Maybe,' her beguiling smile and melting look was beamed in Craig's direction, 'you'll be able to educate me yet in preferring country life to city attractions.'

'Sorry, Jo,' he sounded polite but uninterested, 'but I need Alison with me this time. Special request. Someone's got to stay here with the old lady and keep an eye on her.'

'Can we go with you, Uncle Craig? Can we? Can we?' The twins eyed Craig beseechingly. 'We've only been to a show once,' shouted Patrick. 'Once isn't very much, is it?'

'It'll be on again tomorrow. I'll take you in then.'

'Goody! Goody!' The twins began pushing into their

158

mouths the heaps of green vegetables pushed to the side of their plates.

Jo's face with its dark and angry expression was turned towards Craig. 'I don't see why Alison——'

'I need her to take Banner over the jumps.'

Jo said, 'You mean that white horse up in the paddock, the one you wanted me to learn to ride?'

'That's her, that's Banner. I'd like to see her in the show ring, get a line on whether she goes wild at the sight of the crowd or keeps her head and clears the jumps. She's used to being taken over the hurdles by a girl rider. If only she stays as cool in the arena as she does around here going over the jumps——'

An expression of pride leaped into Alison's eyes. She cried happily, 'Oh, she does! She does!'

Everyone glanced towards her, but she was aware only of Craig's deep intent look. 'How do you know, Alison?'

Too late she realised the blunder into which her own enthusiasm had led her. 'I——' she groped wildly in her mind and came up with something at least feasible. 'I've seen her perform once or twice at shows, down south. At least,' she heard herself babbling wildly, 'it was a white mare and it looked ... like her. I'm sure that her name was Banner.' Beneath Jo's suspicious gaze she could feel the betraying colour rising in her cheeks.

'Well, what d'you know!' disappointment and envy tinged Jo's strong tones. 'Alison has actually told us something about herself. She's been to shows somewhere. At least that's something——'

'Thing is,' Craig cut in smoothly, 'if you could help me out tomorrow with Banner, Alison?' The words were politely spoken, yet somehow, Alison thought in confusion, he made it sound like an order.

Apparently Jo thought so too, for she snapped, 'I don't see why we can't all go tomorrow. Frances could sit in the car and watch——'

'Oh no, dear, I'm afraid not.' Alison had expected Frances to grasp eagerly at an opportunity to leave the house for a time, yet here she was displaying a reluctance to fall in with Jo's suggestion.

'It's my leg,' she explained with a wince of pain. 'It's been playing up all day. I really wouldn't feel like risking a day out, not without checking up with the doctor, and he won't be calling this week. I'm sorry, Jo, but I do need someone at home with me and Alison could do with a break. She's been really housebound lately. It will do her a world of good to get out for a day and forget all about cooking and cleaning and looking after children——'

'She likes us!' wailed Patrick

'Of course I do,' Alison's smile placated the small distressed face. 'I love looking after you both.'

'There's something you've all forgotten,' Jo's voice held a ring of triumph, 'and that is that you won't have any riding gear, Alison. How can you ride in a show? Don't you need jodphurs, hard hat, shirt, jacket, things like that?'

Alison's face fell. It was true. How could she have lost sight of such an essential detail? All she had with her was her beloved saddle.

'It's all right,' Craig spoke with careless confidence. 'It's all taken care of. I've been ringing around the district and got on to the Smiths. Seems they have four daughters, of varying ages but all show-jumpers. They're all married and away now, but their mother told me she has oodles of their gear lying around the place. She's bringing an outfit over tonight.'

'You did?' Alison's face lighted up. She reflected that when it came to Banner's appearance in the show ring at the weekend Craig refused to allow any difficulty to stand in his way. Apparently Jo's thoughts were running along the same lines. She asked curiously, 'How did you know the right size to ask for?'

'I knew.' Craig's gaze was on Alison's face and something deep unspoken yet terribly important passed between them. Like a secret message, she thought, or a caress. Apparently, however, someone else had tuned in on that flash of impact, for Jo was pushing back her chair with a scrape.

'I've had enough!' The chair fell with a crash to the floor, but she left it there and hurried from the room.

Frances from her seat on the settee looked after her worriedly. 'I don't know what made her get so huffy all of a sudden.'

Alison wished she didn't know. In spite of all her resolutions to the contrary a secret traitorous happiness was taking over. Tomorrow ... tomorrow she would be with Craig. She darted a glance towards his impassive face, but he was rolling a cigarette, apparently engrossed in the task. What electricity leaping between them gave her the secret knowledge that, in spite of his calm appearance, he felt it too?

The following afternoon she was on her knees in the back porch, newspapers spread out around her cleaning and polishing her saddle and bridle when Jo came strolling in the door. She said, 'I've just been down to collect the mail,' and something in Jo's tone alerted Alison to danger. There was a malignant sparkle in the prominent blue eyes. Alison turned back to her task. For something to say she murmured, 'Nothing for me?'

'No,' Jo paused at her side, 'but then there wouldn't be any, would there? You never get any mail ever, *and I know why*!'

Alison felt as though someone had punched her in the stomach. So Jo had discovered who she really was and intended to use the knowledge to her advantage. There was no doubt of it, or why did Jo look so triumphant all of a sudden? She bent her head and went on polishing. 'How do you mean?'

'You know what I mean! You're not Alison Wynyard at all! You come from Te-o-nui and you were known there as Alison Carter. You see, I know all about you, how you were forced to give up the house and property when Craig inherited it from the couple who had taken you in.' *Taken her in*, that hurt, that really hurt! Dot and Jim had been her parents in everything but the matter of birth, they had loved her. Had—for all that was over. Now she was on her

161

own and about to be unmasked as a liar and a cheat, even something worse. She could read the accusation in Jo's angry eyes.

'I suppose you thought you were pretty smart, worming your way into Craig's home, making up to him, trying to get him to marry you. Oh, you were determined to get your property back, one way or another, even though it had never ever belonged to you. But Craig wasn't taken in by your schemes and neither was I. It just happened that I was a bit smarter than you. Wait until I tell Craig how you've been pulling the wool over the eyes of everyone here.'

She raised panic-stricken eyes. Her voice was very low. 'How did you find out?'

'It wasn't hard once I got an idea that something was going on.' Jo bent down until her eyes were on a level with Alison's face. Angry, accusing, *triumphant* eyes. 'Last year when I was staying at the house I met an aunt of Craig's. I remembered her telling me about you. She said you had curly red hair and you were engrossing in show-jumping and a white horse you had called Banner. It wasn't much trouble to write away to the aunt and check up on you. I made an excuse that I wanted to buy your mare and needed some details of the owner. I got the answer back today. She fell for the story and told me what she knew. It wasn't much, just that you seemed to have vanished after the house and property were sold up, but that was enough for me. Too bad about your big schemes, but they wouldn't have worked, not with Craig. My advice to you is to get going fast, before I tell everyone here, starting with Craig, how you made a play to get your property back, *the easy way*.'

The colour had drained from Alison's face. She got to her feet. 'You wouldn't!'

'Watch me!' Something about the other girl's set angry face told her Jo would have no hesitation in carrying out her threat. 'It's what you deserve, living a lie like that! Oh, it was a good idea, it might even have worked. You're running enough with that little-girl-lost voice of yours and all the rest of it. I'll keep it to myself, but only if you

162

make yourself scarce. I'll give you until after the weekend and then—out! Is it a deal?'

Alison said very low, 'I can't leave them.'

'Why not? No one is indispensable, especially you. Craig will soon find someone else to give him a hand outside and if he doesn't, I can always help you out. You can easily make some excuse, anything. Tell him you've got a sick mother.'

Alison's winced and Jo had the grace to look a little ashamed. 'Tell him anything, I don't care, as long as you get going!'

Alison's thoughts were whirling in turmoil. Why did her presence here mean so much to Jo? She couldn't be jealous, not on her account—or could she? Should she make a confession to Craig herself, tell him who she was and how it had all happened that she found herself here? Would he believe her? It was scarcely likely, because Jo would leave him in no doubt as to the truth or otherwise of the story. He would be told that she had been pursuing him for her own gains and anything would be preferable to that, even flight. Frances won't need me here in a matter of a week or two and the twins will soon forget. Craig . . . but it didn't do to think of Craig. She would like him to remember her once in a while, remember her not as a scheming little money-grabber but just . . . Alison.

'Well,' demanded Jo harshly, 'have you made up your mind? What's it to be?'

Alison said slowly, 'I haven't any choice, have I?' The words were rung from some deep well of pain. 'Not really.'

'Hello, what goes on?' Craig, looking happy and carefree, pushed his felt sombrero to the back of his head as he came whistling up the path. 'You two are looking pretty intent on something or other. What is it, girl's talk?'

Alison didn't dare look up for fear he would glimpse the anguish in her face. It was Jo's cool tones that made answer. 'Something like that. You wouldn't be interested.'

'How do you know?' He went on into the house and Jo followed him.

163

Alison gathered up polish and brushes and stowed them in her woven flax pipi-kit. Now hat she had lost everything and her last hope of happiness had fled a wild recklessness took over. She had a day, one day left from the wreckage of all those crazy dreams. Even Jo couldn't cheat her out of those few hours alone with Craig away from the other girl's jealous accusing eyes.

As she took saddle and bridle into the shed she made up her mind that tomorrow she and Banner would give their best performance ever! Banner ... the thought struck her with a sense of loss that she could never claim her mare now. Faced with that deeper deprivation, however, even the prospect of losing Banner faded into insignificance.

All at once she realised that Craig was moving towards her. 'Here, let me do that.' He lifted the saddle up to a bracket. 'All set for tomorrow?'

She nodded, unable to trust herself to speak, thankful that in the dimness of the old shed he couldn't see the tears that blinded her eyes.

Nonchalantly he leaned against a shelf, his gaze on her averted face. 'How was the gear from Smiths? Fit okay?'

'Oh yes, yes!' She prayed he wouldn't catch the unsteady note in her voice, 'I tried it all on last night and even the jodphur boots were the right size. I don't know how you knew——'

'Don't you?' The caressing note in his low tones went straight to her heart. His gaze rested on the slim young figure and turned-away face and she felt his hand on her head, ruffling the tumbled curls. 'I know a whole lot about you, Alison.'

She gave a shaky laugh. Thank heaven he didn't!

All at once his tone was casual. 'We'll load Banner on to the truck early, about seven—did you want something, Jo?'

'Nothing.' Jo's glance darted from his laconic face to Alison's tremulous lips. 'Just a handkerchief. I must have left it somewhere else.'

CHAPTER TEN

ALISON slept little that night and it was a relief to get up very early in the morning, a day of soft cloud where, as so often in this part of the country, sky, sea and land mingled in an atmospheric effect. The rain that hovered near yet never seemed to fall hovered overhead in grey cottonwool clouds streaked with sunshine. Like my life, Alison mused. So soon she would be parted from Craig for ever, but today was her own, shot with golden gleams of excitement.

When she went to catch Banner to groom her for the show the mare was already at the gate nickering to her as she approached. Yesterday she had worked up a soapy lather and rubbed it into the white coat. Now, however, it was clear that the mare had rolled in the grass, for the white legs were stained with green. 'Oh, Banner, how *could* you?' Alison scrubbed the legs down, plaited the neatly trimmed mane and tail and rubbed oil into the hooves.

She returned to the house to change into the borrowed riding gear, now pressed and immaculate. The bald patches on the hard hat she had touched up with black boot polish, a trick she had often resorted to in the past. When she was dressed and ready she was struck once again by the perfect fit of the garments. Who would have guessed that Craig would be so observant concerning herself? Thinking of Craig brought back the surge of wild inexplicable happiness that had besumed her at intervals since yesterday. He's only taking you to a local show, she reminded herself, and that only because of Banner. Didn't he tell you that he wants to try her out against competition? There's nothing personal in his invitation, how could there be?

So why did she feel this way? It was no use, no amount of rationalising could avail against the high tide of excitement and anticipation, and all the time the feeling of recklessness persisted. She was tired of pretending, sickened of being treated by Jo as someone who apart from her duties was of little account in the household.

Presently, in jodphurs, white blouse and green tie with the bright curls brushed away from her face, she went out to help load Banner into the waiting truck. Craig was there already, freshly-shaven, oddly unfamiliar and terribly attractive in lemon shirt, checked sports jacket and slacks. Or was it the expression in his eyes when he greeted her that was throwing her into this state of wild confusion?

'I'm so lucky you got me the gear to wear today,' she told him breathlessly, 'though I still don't know how you guessed the size so perfectly.'

'I told you, I notice everything about you—especially the way your hair curls up like this.' Once again he put up a hand to touch the coppery-red waves and curls. 'Don't put the helmet on yet. Why hide hair like that?'

Because this was dangerous territory in which she couldn't afford to linger she said hurriedly, 'The truck would hold a couple of horses.' She remembered the glittering array of silver trophies arranged along the mantel. 'Why not change your mind and enter for some events yourself today?'

'Can't do that. Sabre's let me down badly, he got caught up in some barbed wire last night and ripped a nasty gash in his leg. I'll get the vet to come and have a look at him. Anyway, its your day today, Alison!'

'And Banner's!' He didn't appear to hear her.

Although in the past when taking Banner to shows and gymkhanas the mare had been no problem at all to get into the horse float, today she showed a reluctance to enter the truck. At last, however, with a lot of heaving and pushing, plus appeals by Alison and a certain amount of strong language on Craig's part, they got her up the ramp and into the vehicle.

A hurried cup of coffee and slice of toast at the house, then they collected the picnic hamper Alison had prepared in readiness for the outing and they were out in the yard

166

once again. The others were still in bed, but the twins wandered out in their sleeping suits, watching with interest as Alison climbed up to the high seat and Craig secured the doors of the vehicle.

'Goodbye! Goodbye!' The children were still waving enthusiastically when Alison got out of the truck to open the last gate before they turned into the main road.

'It seems mean not taking them with us,' she murmured as she climbed back into the truck.

'Take them!' Craig threw an incredulous glance. 'After all the trouble I've been to to get you to myself for once.'

Her pulses leaped, then steadied, and she glanced towards him uncertainly. He didn't mean what he'd said, of course, it was all just a game to him, part of the day's outing. 'You're joking!'

'I never lie to you, Alison,' his voice softened, deepened. 'If you like I'll prove it to you.'

Again the wild sweet happiness. 'I believe you,' she said hastily. And so she did—almost. No doubt he did mean what he said, at the moment. To change the subject she said, 'Tell me about the place where the show is being held. Is it far?'

'Roughly an hour and a half's drive from here. It's an annual event and from what I gather they get a great attendance. They tell me the crowds get bigger every year and so do the show attractions. There'll be the usual chop, merry-go-round and all that stuff for the kids, with a rodeo on the second day. The ads feature something new to me. Seems a farmer somewhere up north has kept some bullocks and trained them as a team. Quite a novelty these days. Ever come across a bullock team in your part of the country?'

'No.' Any mention of her past life brought with it a feeling of defensiveness that was becoming a habit with her. Wait for it. Next would come the inevitable query, 'Where *do* you come from, Alison? You've never really let on.'

Surprisingly, however, he did not pursue the subject and she relaxed in her seat. 'Will you buy me some candy floss when we get there, Craig? I've got a weakness for it.'

He slanted her a teasing grin. 'Not that sticky pink tack? You don't mean to tell me you like it?'

'Love it.'

'It's just a lot of nothing.'

Like my happy day with you, Craig, that seems so perfect, yet underneath it's all as unsubstantial and airy-fairy as candy floss. 'I like it,' she persisted stubbornly.

'Then you shall have it. And anything else you want.'

Anything else? Oh, Craig, don't torture me. She forced her mind back to her surroundings. To the long straight bordered with raupo and blowing flax and the green hills all around them with their long shadows chased by the wind. Craig was driving carefully with concern for the mare and as they went on they could glimpse in the distance a Land Rover towing a horse-float, followed by a long stock truck and trailer. Other vehicles too were heading in the direction of the show grounds. Above them the swiftly-changing skies were darkening. Great gun-metal clouds collided with a thunderous roar and big drops splashed against the dust of the windscreen. Another minute and rain streamed down the windows. Alison, peering ahead, could scarcely see ahead because the road was almost obliterated by the sudden deluge. Then as abruptly as it had started the pelting cyclonic downpour cleared, the clouds drifted away and the sun was shining hotly, adding a fresh sparkle to tea-tree and flax that lined the roadside.

They passed through a small country township where modern attractive shops lined the main street, sped past a picturesque old timber hotel, a petrol pump on the corner. Ahead of them was a long line of vehicles and clustered around the entrance gates of the large area of the showgrounds were trucks and Land Rovers, horse floats and stock carriers. As they took the track towards the grassy enclosure where horses and vehicles were assembled Alison caught glimpses of tents and open stalls. She watched the ferris wheel as it circled high in a washed blue sky and heard the carnival music grinding out from the merry-go-round where excited children clung shrieking to their wooden mounts. Then Craig was guiding the truck in a space between the parked caravans and tethered horses. To Alison it was a familiar scene with children anxiously attending to their ponies, parents hovering around cars and horse-floats, a voice on a loudspeaker calling for competitors entered in a pony event.

Craig led Banner from the truck and tethered her to the side of the vehicle. 'I'll go and put in your entry. What's it to be?'

She glanced up from grooming the mare. The mood of recklessness still possessed her and she looked back at him levelly. 'The Champion Hunter of course, what else? She can do it!'

The expression of pride and excitement that crossed his face was worth a lot. 'That's my girl!'

Oddly she didn't feel in the least perturbed in anticipation of competing in the champion show-jumping event of the afternoon. It was that sort of day when anything could happen. And Banner, she knew, was an outstanding show-jumper.

When Craig had moved away in the direction of a tent where two women were taking names for the hack ring events, Alison took her saddle and bridle from the truck. She had complete faith in Banner, especially as she knew she could trust her mount not to allow excitement to get the better of her. Had Craig but known, the mare was quite at home amongst the crowds and general bustle of the show. Hadn't Banner won for herself endless rosettes, red ribbons and silver trophies at similar gatherings over the past few years? Not the Champion Hunter event—well, not yet, but Alison was going to see that today Banner gave it a darn good try!

What puzzled her was that Craig showed no surprise at her confidence in the mare's jumping ability. Another odd thing was the confidence he appeared to have in her as a rider. One would have expected him to question her regarding previous events in which she had taken part, but he hadn't done that. Had she not known such a thing was well nigh impossible she might almost have suspected him of knowing all about her. At the thought her heart almost stopped. Then she told herself not to be absurd. How could he know? For a moment she stood motionless. *I wish he did know. I wish there was nothing between us, no secrets, no Jo.*

'It's all fixed.' Craig came striding towards her over the wet grass. 'Your event isn't on until late.' How happy and animated he looked! Much too happy for a man parted from his love? Nonsense, he was merely enjoying the day, excited over the possibilities of the performance of the white mare in the show ring, for it was clear that his faith in Banner's show-jumping abilities matched her own, and she *knew* what Banner could do. Of course that was the explanation of his high spirits. 'You'll have swags of competition,' he told her as he came back to join her. 'There's a mob of entries for that event and the jumps are high, particularly the brush ones. Come along and take a look.' He tucked her arm in his and they threaded their way between parked caravans and stock trailers as they moved towards the arena. For a time they stood watching the entrants assemble for the next event but Alison was aware only of Craig's nearness, his touch. Presently they moved away to the roped-off area separating the hack and pony rings, Alison, however, was finding it difficult to concentrate on the field. She was much too conscious of his nearness and it was only vaguely that she realised that the brush jumps were high indeed and so was the wire jump in the centre of the field. A tiny voice that she knew she shouldn't trust echoed deep in her mind. As though anything could go wrong today!

They watched the event, waiting as the judges adjudicated points and announced the winners. Then they turned their attention to the field on the opposite side of the track where children mounted on ponies were moving in a ring. One small girl with a mop of red ringlets was evidently finding difficulty in controlling her restive mount, because she trailed a long way behind her competitors.

'She looks like you,' observed Craig. 'All those curls—or weren't you like that at eight years old?'

Alison laughed. 'I guess I could have been—a bit. I know I was about that age when I first started taking my pony to the local show.' *Careful now*, Alison.

He didn't follow the lead she had given him, thank heaven. She said smilingly, 'I hope I give a better account of myself today than that!' For the small rider had slipped to the ground and was sobbing bitterly.

'You will.' It was amazing, the confidence he had in her considering that all he had to go on was seeing her clear the farm fences or take Banner over the jumps she had made for herself in the paddock.

As they made their way amongst happy family groups and excited children Alison mused that it was fortunate both she and Craig were strangers to the district. Otherwise they may have found themselves drawn into a picnic party or a group of young farmers. But they strolled on unchallenged until suddenly raindrops pelted down once again and they hurried back to the shelter of the truck. Alison didn't mind rain today, not when it meant she could sit in the front of the vehicle with Craig, screened from everyone by the cyclonic shower. All at once it was over, the sun struggled through cloud and once again everything was a-glitter.

In the fitful sunshine they dropped down from the truck and hand in hand like children, they leaped over rain puddles on the path as they made their way towards a wood-chopping event in the ring at the entrance to the pavilion. They watched as one competitor after another mounted a tree to wield a flashing axe with speed and precision as the chips fell around. At last they moved on, passing the sheep pens under the trees and the sheep-shearing pavilion where muscular men with sweat running down their shoulders worked against the clock as the heavy fleeces fell to the floor. Then they wandered away to watch the teams of marching girls, preceded by a military band playing from the cramped shelter of the official stand. Still hand in hand they stood watching the grand parade headed by a team of bullocks patiently plodding around the ring. Behind them came the glossy horses and prize-winning stock, then the cars, tractors and motor cycles on display.

When it was over they strolled towards the stalls, mingling with the crowd while the age-old carnival melodies around them formed a background to all the fun of the fair. Craig bought a hot-dog for himself, but when he asked Alison to have one too she shook her head. 'You promised——'

'Oh yes, the candy floss.' They found a tent nearby where a girl was bending over the whirling candy in a drum and he presented Alison with a cornet of pink fluff.

They returned to watch the riding events in the ring until the announcer declared a break for lunch and they made their way back to the truck. The day, her precious day, was flying by so fast!

With appetites sharpened by the fresh air they enjoyed the man-sized hamburgers Alison had prepared. The freshly-baked buns filled with ham and salad were a welcome change from the usual diet of mutton which she prepared in various ways. Afterwards she poured coffee from a flask and they bit into crunchy red apples plucked from trees in the orchard that morning.

When the show-jumper events were resumed Craig helped her to saddle Banner. Alison leaped up lightly, and waited for the signal to enter the arena. It came at last and as she alerted the mare Craig was beside her, his hand warm and encouraging as he clasped her fingers. 'Good luck, Alison!'

'Thanks, Craig.' He came with her as she rode Banner towards the high brush jumps. As she warmed her own mount up other riders entered one at a time. One horse, excited by the crowd and waving flags, shied away from the first fence. A big bay hunter refused suddenly at the huge brush, tipping his rider on to the ground. She realised it would not be easy. There had been no clear rounds at all.

CHAPTER ELEVEN

'ALISON Wynyard!' She heard her own name called, the name to which she was getting accustomed. No longer did she do a double-take before realising it was her own. As she entered the grassy enclosure the look on Craig's face stayed with her. When he looked at her like that she felt she could do anything, anything!

The confidence born of the moment persisted. Or could it be pride in her mount that prompted this feeling of assurance? For Banner, with her long steady stride and unflappable nature, was progressing without a fault. As one brush jump after another loomed up she took exactly the right sized stride beforehand, then spreading herself out, sailed over, to land perfectly on the other side. The crowd that had gathered to witness the main event of the day crowded close to the rope. As Alison swept around once again she was tempted to look, for Craig for she knew he would be watching her progress, but long training held and she fixed her gaze ahead on the high brush jump.

Over ... then another ... over ... no trouble at all. Now there remained only the last hurdle, the wire jump in the centre of the field, to surmount. A hush fell over the watching crowd as the girl mounted on the graceful white mare moved towards the final jump, a coppery-haired girl who was leaning forward in the saddle. She could feel Banner gathering herself and spreading out. They were up, up and over, a faultless performance completing a clear round.

A cheer broke from the crowd as Alison on Banner cantered away, but she was scarcely aware of the groups pressed against the rope barrier. She only knew that Craig was there, Craig looking at her in a way he had never done before, elated, with wildly shining eyes. He hurried towards her and as she slipped down from the saddle he caught her close. 'You made it, Alison! You made it! I knew you would!' His eyes said a lot more, said things she dared not interpret. *Why fool yourself, it's Banner's success he's so excited about!*

She became aware that strangers were approaching her, offering congratulations, shaking her by the hand. It was a victory for her and Banner—not the one she wanted, but nevertheless a victory, and there was no doubt they meant it kindly.

'Good show!'

'Great performance you put up, Miss Wynyard!'

'Have you shown Banner often?'

'What else have you won with her?'

The questions and congratulations fell around her until the voice of the judge echoing over the loudspeaker called her away. 'The winner of the Champion Hunter Event is Alison Wynyard on Banner. The prize is a cheque for seventy dollars as well as a silver cup donated by Lord Westerbury of England.'

Alison moved forward to accept the trophy and prize money. She thanked the sponsors and the judge. Then when the prizegiving was over she made her way back to Craig, waiting on the outskirts of the crowd. They were examining the silver trophy together when the judge, a tall alert-looking woman of middle age, walked across the grass to join them.

'That's a great mare you've got there!' she said to Alison. 'I can't think why I didn't recognise her right away. This is the second time I've awarded her first place in a hunter event. Last year at a gymkhana in Te-o-nui, remember? It was your name that put me off the track. Alison Wynyard was unfamiliar.' Her friendly glance went to Craig, standing tall and attentive at Alison's side. 'I didn't know you were married, my dear. This is your husband?'

To Alison the terrible shame-making moment seemed to last for ever. 'No,' she gasped, 'I——'

Something of her distress must have got through to the woman. She said quickly, 'I just took it for granted. I'm

174

afraid I've made an awful mistake——'

'No mistake,' Craig's cool tones cut across the embarrassed accents. 'You're a bit early, that's all. Carter's my name, and I'm going to make it Alison's too——'

'*Carter*?' The expression of the judge's sun-weathered face changed from one of surprise to complete bewilderment. 'But that was—I don't get it.'

'You will!' Craig assured her in his easy tone.

'Sorry to butt in,' a man in riding gear touched the woman on the arm, 'but they're waiting for you in the judge's tent——'

'Not to worry,' Craig told her with his friendly grin, 'we'll explain it all later. Better still, we'll send you an invitation to the wedding!'

'Wedding!' Alison tried to speak lightly, but she didn't make much of a success of it. How much had Craig understood of the judge's words? Enough to make him realise that she was living under an assumed name, or what must appear to him to be an assumed name. 'That poor woman,' she was speaking wildly, running on in panic, 'she won't be in a fit state to do any more judging today with you spinning her a tale like that.'

'But we *are* getting married—if you'll have me!' He spoke so softly, yet all around her bells seemed to be ringing. The next moment she came back to reality with a jolt.

He was teasing her, of course. His talk of marriage had been an impulse thought up on the spur of the moment to cover her obvious dismay and confusion, what else? He couldn't really mean it. All at once she felt utterly deflated. 'You don't understand, what she said about me is true. Here, take these——' she thrust towards him the silver trophy and the cheque. It was finished, this stupid masquerade of hers, all over in one minute. She pulled herself up in the saddle, said wretchedly, 'You see, I did have another name when I was given a red rosette at a gymkhana last year.' She pulled on the rein.

'I know,' he said calmly, 'it was Carter.'

'You—knew?' She spun around, incredulous.

He took hold of the bridle and there was no avoiding his direct gaze. 'I've known about you for a long time.'

'But how——? I didn't say a word.'

'Didn't you?' It was odd, but he didn't appear disillusioned and angry or even disgusted with her. And how calm was his tone, she thought bewilderedly, not at all the sort of reaction one would have expected from him now that her trickery had been exposed. She wrenched her mind back to the deep tones.

'Remember the night of the smash? The time you flaked out when I was taking you home? You gave yourself away, you know, you told me yourself.'

Her eyes were wide in dismay. 'But I couldn't have!' she cried incredulously. 'I didn't say anything.'

'You said it all in five little words. "Take me home to Te-o-nui." '

'And that was how you knew?'

A twinkle of amusement flickered in his eyes. 'Oh, there were plenty of pointers along the way. Remember that first day when you caught sight of Banner? No girl would get all that excited over a strange white mare. And Banner's welcome to you was pretty obvious too. Besides, you did clam up every time I brought up anything to do with your past life. You looked guilty as hell into the bargain. I told you,' he reminded her gently, 'that your face is a dead giveaway every time!'

'But I didn't know,' she told him in her sweet young voice. 'I had no idea when I called at your place with Mary that it was *your* home. Truly, Craig, you've just *got* to believe me!'

For a moment he was silent, regarding her with an expression she couldn't interpret.

'I didn't go there for the reason you think,' she cried defensively, and felt the hot colour flooding her cheeks. 'You don't need to feel——'

'Come on, Alison,' he said softly, 'take Banner away

176

and give her a drink and a brush-down. Then we'll shove her back in the truck and take off.'

'Take off?' Her spirits plummeted. He had hidden his feelings well, but underneath it all it was all too clear that he couldn't wait to be rid of her. Dispiritedly she turned away.

Suddenly his compelling tones were deep with emotion. 'We'll go somewhere where I can tell you how I feel about you.'

Alison began to tremble inside. He didn't speak like a man who never wished to set eyes on her again. *Could he possibly have meant those words about a wedding?* The next moment she wrenched her mind back to sanity. Things like that didn't really happen.

When they reached the grassy enclosure competitors who had been taking part in the jumping and flat events were already loading their mounts into trucks and horse-floats, coloured ribbons fluttering from the cabs of vehicles. To everyone else as well as Craig this was no more than the end of an enjoyable day, while to Alison it meant the end of everything she held dear.

Heavy-hearted, she led Banner up the ramp and into the truck, tossing the silver trophy carelessly on to the seat. What matter a silver cup now that she had lost the real prize in life?

'Why so sad?' Seated in the high seat at her side, Craig had his hand on the starter. Was it his uncanny perception concerning herself or that too-revealing face of hers that enabled him to divine her feelings so correctly?

Hastily she composed her features into a pleasant mask. 'I'm not really.' She gazed unseeingly out of the window. The giant ferris wheel was stilled, a tracery against a grey sky, and the muddied pathway leading to the gates ahead was jammed with slow-moving trucks and transporters, horse-floats and dust-spattered cars.

At length they were out on the main road joining in a long procession of vehicles winding in the direction of a small township ahead. As they came nearer she could

177

glimpse water tumbling over a rocky cliff into a river below and presently they were approaching a small colourful township with hilly streets and clean attractive stores that lined the highway. As Craig pulled up in the main street she glanced across at him in surprise. 'Why are we stopping here?'

He didn't answer for a moment. A look of controlled excitement flickered in the dark blue eyes, excitement ... and something else. Alison said uncertainly, 'Is there something you want?'

'*Is* there?' How strange he sounded, so quiet and intense, as if it were something that mattered terribly to him, something like—— Again the look of secret excitement that made her heart give a crazy upsurge. Was it possible that incredible story he had told the woman judge hadn't been just a fun-thing after all, could he really have meant it for real? The next moment she pulled herself up. He was probably referring to some part of machinery he needed for the truck or tractor which he intended buying from the garage opposite. There she went again, reading impossible things into his gaze.

'I'm hoping I'll get what I want tonight. Let's see, shall we?'

Obligingly she leaped lightly down on to the footpath and once again Craig clasped her hand in his. 'Come on, this happens to be important!' It *must* be a part for the truck.

They waited while a great stock-transporter thundered past then he led her into the door of a restaurant. She looked up at him in surprise. 'But you said——'

'Let's eat first.' Once again she was aware of his air of suppressed excitement.

She hesitated. 'What about the others at home? Jo——'

'Forget about Jo!' *Forget about Jo!* Alison could scarcely believe her ears. 'This is our night, just us, you and me.'

So the day wasn't yet finished after all, the magic still endured. Why not take the reprieve she had been offered, multiply the memories? Another hour or so with him would be something to remember in the lonely years that stretched ahead. She preceded him down the long carpeted aisle of the dimly-lighted room and without waiting for the waitress who was moving towards them he led Alison to an isolated table in a quiet corner away from the main body of diners. He saw her seated, then flung himself down opposite her, handing her the menu. 'The fried schnapper they put on here is recommended, probably caught this morning right here in the harbour.'

'That'll be fine.' At this moment she couldn't have cared less what variety of food was served to her. It would all taste heavenly, eaten here with Craig. All at once it came to her how seldom they had been alone together during the past week or so. Her own fault really, seeing that since Jo's arrival at the house she had resisted all attempts by Craig to speak with her in private. Tonight was different, tonight she would take what fate offered.

He gave the order and when the wine steward approached their table, ordered champagne.

'Champagne?' At her expression of surprise he leaned over the table, his eyes dark and intent. 'Why not? It's a celebration. Special!'

Then she remembered. Of course, he was referring to the Champion Hunter trophy she had won today.

Mindful of the mare waiting in the truck outside, they did not linger over the meal. When they emerged from the resturant the amethyst haze over the hills had darkened to a soft darkness, pricked with a handful of stars. As she climbed back into the truck Alison reflected that she was glad they had interrupted the journey to eat at the restaurant. It had given her a little more time and, for her, time was running out. As they moved away into the night Craig threw an arm around her shoulders and she found herself wishing the journey could last for ever. At intervals they passed clusters of lights that were small townships along the highway, then all too soon they had left the smooth bitumen and had turned into a rough metal road, where the only sign of habitation was the glow of an isolated farmhouse set high on a hill. Presently she caught the glimmer of lake water at the side of the road and before long the sombre pine forests rising on either side of the winding track told her they were nearing their destination.

She was very quiet as they approached the turn-off and soon she was getting out to open the gates. When Craig pulled up in the yard she slipped down from the high seat and soon they were unloading Banner. Alison led the mare away while Craig garaged the truck.

The moon had risen, a silver ball in a luminous dark-blue sky. In the moonglow she led the mare up the silvered pathway winding up the slope. As she closed the gate in the paddock a dark shadow was coming towards her and a moment later Craig was beside her ... a different Craig this ... 'Alison!' He caught her close and kissed her forehead, the tip of her nose, her throat, and last of all, her lips. At last he released her, whispered hoarsely, 'I've wanted to do this for a long time, but you never gave me the chance——'

The poignant forbidden happiness was taking over. 'I know I know——' Then sanity came back with a rush. 'But Jo——'

He caught her once more in strong arms, holding her closer than ever. 'You can forget about Jo, put her right out of your mind——'

She stirred, said on a sigh, 'If only I could!'

'It's over, my sweet. Whatever there was between us is dead and gone.' His wild exultant laugh echoed in her ears as once again his seeking lips were on her own.

When she could speak ... 'Over!' Dazedly she stared up at him, unable to take in the electrifying words he had said. 'You mean, there's nothing between you and her?'

'I mean there never was anything real with Jo and me, and whatever there was was all washed up a long time ago. It was a bit difficult ... I was hoping she would get the message and shoot back to the South where she comes from, but in the end I had to spell it out, tell her the truth. I guess she had to have it straight, especially as she was spreading the word around about staying on with me for good.'

He drew a little away, his eyes dark and thoughtful. 'We had it all out last night, late. It wasn't too pleasant, but there were things that had to be got out in the open. I don't think she was too surprised really. She must have known we were through with each other a year ago. That was the reason she took off on the tourist trip. I happen to know that she was planning a wedding when she got back from the cruise, an Australian she'd met on the trip. But something happened, a story got around that he already had a girl of his own back in Sydney. Anyway, Jo found herself out on a limb. It was a situation she couldn't take. Her pride had taken a pounding and she got the idea of salvaging something out of the wreck of our old relationship, such as it was. There was a time when just for a while——' He broke off. 'No need to go into that. Jo would never have meant anything to me, even if I hadn't been lucky enough to meet you.'

His words were ringing bells again all over the place.

'Did Jo ... say anything about me?'

'Oh, she tried to tell me some story about you and your name, nothing I hadn't known already.'

Alison stirred in his arms. 'You didn't think I'd done it deliberately, coming here, I mean?' and held her breath for the answer.

'I—know—you, Alison.' His kisses punctuated the words. 'Jo's raking up the old ashes didn't mean a thing to me. She'll thank me one of these days when she meets someone more in her own line. The country life was not for her, or a country man either.' His voice softened, deepened. 'Not like my girl.'

'What is she like?' Alison whispered.

'Oh, she's really something! I was so lucky to find her! So pretty ... so very lovely ...' He twined around his finger a clinging copper-coloured tendril of hair. 'You wouldn't believe that a girl so lovely could be so know-ledgeable.'

She raised a flushed face. 'Only because I like working with you.'

He said softly, 'There's more to marriage than work, you know.'

'Marriage?'

'I've had it on my mind for quite a while,' he whispered close to her ear. 'There's just one real love in my life, and I've found it right here amongst the sandhills. Once you came into my life, that was it!' All at once the deep tones were warm and tender. He caught her closer and once again his lips sought hers. 'Marry me, say you'll marry me and I'll never have to let you go again—ever.'

'The answer's "yes",' she whispered, the remainder of the words lost in his caress. She was swept by elation she had never known existed. The stars seemed to be whirling overhead and her whole being rose on a great wave of happiness.

After a time she murmured contentedly, 'If only I'd known that with you there was no secret to worry about!' She stirred in his arms, reaching up to trace the lines of the beloved masculine face. 'Why didn't you let on when you first knew about me?'

He put her fingers to his lips. 'I wasn't going to risk losing you. I was all set to get things cleared up as soon as you were well again after the accident. Then Jo breezed in to ruin everything and I didn't want to push my luck. I knew what might happen if I let on to you about knowing all about you right then, with Jo talking about house alterations, making out everything was set and all she had to do was plan the wedding. You'd have taken off, you know you would, and I'd have had to go and find you all over again. The way I looked at it it was easier to let things ride, mark time until I got matters straightened out with Jo.' Once again his kiss started a trembling in her. 'Everything sorted out now?'

'Oh yes, yes,' she whispered. 'It's so wonderful to have no more secrets, especially your knowing about my coming here being a mere accident——' She raised a tremulous face. 'You do believe me?'

'Not really.' She caught his low exultant laugh. 'I'd call it fate!'

Alison felt inclined to agree with the verdict. 'You knew, though,' she murmured, 'the moment I mentioned Te-o-nui?'

He held her close. 'There's only one place of that name I've ever heard of, only one girl with coppery-coloured hair, a girl called Alison, who disappeared from there, vanished so completely that my inquiries with her lawyer came to a dead end and all my letters failed to catch up with her. They were sent back to me by the Post Office, address unknown.'

'You wrote to me?'

'Half a dozen times. I wanted you to share the inheritance with me. I made it plain that we'd be partners—but now,' passion and urgency were in his kiss, 'I've found a better way. That's why I'm asking you to stay with me for ever.' His hand traced her soft cheek. 'I love you.' Then she was caught in his arms, close, close. His voice came muffled, hoarse with emotion. 'Right from the start when you walked into my life I couldn't think of anything else, I couldn't get you out of my mind. The thoughts of you going out with young Nick nearly sent me raving mad.'

'You needn't have worried. How do you think I felt when Jo turned up out of the blue?'

'Oh, Jo.' The lack of interest in his tone told her how mistaken she had been in ever imagining that any embers remained from forgotten fires. The next moment he whispered close to her ear, 'There never was anyone else but you, there never will be.'

'Me too.' She had no doubts, no fears, only this rapturous sense of happiness and fulfilment.

'It's you and me together from now on.' All at once his tone softened. 'It's a pretty rugged life you'll be taking on with me, little one, especially when a man happens to be working on his own. There'll be times when I'll have to call on you to give me a hand with mustering. You'll need to cook for gangs of shearers as well as feed all the other bods that turn up to stay. Farm cadets, duck-shooters, wild pig hunters, the odd fisherman——'

Alison put a hand to his lips. 'I'll love it all—with you.'

When she could think constructively once again she murmured, 'I wonder what Frances will say when she hears our news? I know she'll be surprised——'

'You reckon?' Amusement tinged his tone. 'The old lady's been on at me from almost the first day you arrived at the house about not letting you slip away. It wasn't Jo whom she'd picked out for a daughter-in-law, not once she'd met you.'

'Jo——' she linked the bronzed fingers in her own, 'she really did seem to think she'd be your wife before long——'

For a moment Craig's face sobered. 'She'll get over it. Don't worry about her.'

Alison was too wildly happy to feel over-concerned about the other girl. 'She did *try*.'

'She didn't have a hope.' The restless wind endlessly blowing over dark sandhills ruffled his soft dark hair and tossed her clustered curls back from her forehead as once again he bent to kiss her. 'Let's go and tell the old lady. You know what she'll say, don't you?'

Alison laughed softly. 'How about, "Blame it on the soft west wind of love?" '

When they went into the house a light burned in Frances' bedroom and together they went into the room.

Frances, who was sitting up in bed, put down the detective novel she had been reading.

'We've got something to tell you,' Craig said.

His mother's gaze went from Alison, flushed with excitement and happiness, to the unmistakable expression of pride on her son's lean face. His arm thrown lightly around Alison's waist, he drew her close and there was no mistaking the depth of feeling in his low exultant tones. 'Alison isn't leaving here ever, are you, sweet?'

Her denial was a tremulous whisper. 'We wanted you to be the first to know.'

'But that's wonderful news!' An expression of incredulous delight rang in Frances' strong tones. Her eyes suffused with most un-Frances-like tears of emotion. 'Alison dear, I just can't tell you how pleased I am about this!' Throwing back the covers, she jumped out of bed. Her long nightgown flapped around her ankles as she ran across the room and throwing her arms around Alison kissed her heartily. When she had assured Alison over and over again of her delight in gaining the daughter-in-law she wanted she crossed to the wardrobe and taking out a serviceable red woollen dressing gown, pulled it around her.

'Oh dear,' she clapped a weather-roughened hand to her mouth. 'I almost forgot. It's Jo! She's gone! She came in to see me just after you two had left the house this morning and told me she had just had an urgent message calling her back to the South Island.' Frances' eyes were thoughtful. 'Funny, I didn't hear the phone ring. Anyway, she came out of her room carrying her suitcase, rang for a taxi at Dargaville to come and collect her and just—went. She didn't even say goodbye to the twins. She just took off.'

Alison's gaze went to Craig and his glance signalled back a message. You see, it's all over. You've nothing more to worry about from Jo.

Alison let out her breath on a long sigh of relief, but on another level something clicked in her mind. What was it Frances had said about the children? 'The twins—who's been looking after them all day?'

'I have.' Frances gave her a rakish grin. 'They were no trouble at all, the darlings!'

'Frances, you're a fraud! You're walking around all over the place without even a limp. Know what I think? You've been up and about for the last couple of weeks, when no one was looking.' Enlightenment dawned on her. 'So that was why you wouldn't let us call the doctor to come and see you for a final check-up?'

'She's right, you know,' joined in Craig. 'You may as well

185

come clean and tell us about it now that you've given yourself away. What was the idea of putting one across us, making out you were a helpless invalid? It couldn't be that you liked being waited on hand and foot by Alison, I know you better than that.'

'I had my reasons.' Frances couldn't quite hide the expression of smug satisfaction that had spread over her craggy features. 'How else,' she demanded of her son, 'could I get Alison to stay on? I had to think up something to keep her here until you came to your senses and did something about asking her to stay on for ever. You see, I knew,' she added complacently, 'that it was just a matter of time.' She swung around to Alison. 'You will forgive me for my little deception, won't you, love?'

'*Forgive you*?' Alison laughed her clear young laugh with the catch in her throat. 'It's the best thing anyone has ever done for me in my whole life. Talking of deceptions, her dancing glance went to Craig's glowing face, 'shall we tell her?'

His eyes were tender, loving, amused.

'Might as well. You'll never keep anything from the old lady for long.'

Frances glanced bewilderedly from one to the other. 'Tell me what, for heaven's sake?'

'Just,' explained Craig with a grin, 'that her name happens to be Carter already. Alison Carter—does it ring a bell with you?'

Frances gasped. 'You don't mean *that* Alison Carter?'

It took quite a time to explain the whole story, but at last Frances understood all that had happened. Moving to a drawer, she began rummaging amongst the oddments for pad and ballpoint.

'Another proverb?' Alison asked smilingly.

'Oh no, dear, not this time. I've just been thinking about the wedding. We'll have it from here, of course. Just a small affair. Mary could be your bridesmaid. You did say you have no folks of your own?'

Alison flushed and smiling, glanced from Craig, his eyes

186

warm with love and tenderness, to Frances' weatherbeaten face. 'Oh, but I have!' she protested. 'I've got all I want,' she murmured contentedly, 'right here.'

When they had left the room Craig said softly, 'I should have warned you that the old lady would start thinking up names for wedding invitations the minute we passed on the news. Do you mind?'

'I don't mind.' All that mattered to her was Craig, close at her side, loving her, needing her—for keeps.

Did you miss any of these exciting Harlequin Omnibus 3-in-1 volumes?

Each volume contains 3 great novels
by one author for only $1.95.
See order coupon.

Violet Winspear #3
The Cazalet Bride
(#1434)
Beloved Castaway
(#1472)
The Castle of the
Seven Lilacs (#1514)

Anne Mather
Charlotte's Hurricane
(#1487)
Lord of Zaracus (#1574)
The Reluctant Governess
(#1600)

Anne Hampson

Anne Hampson #1
Unwary Heart (#1388)
Precious Waif (#1420)
The Autocrat of Melhurst
(#1442)

Betty Neels

Betty Neels
Tempestuous April
(#1441)
Damsel in Green (#1465)
Tulips for Augusta
(#1529)

Essie Summers

Essie Summers #3
Summer in December
(#1416)
The Bay of the
Nightingales (#1445)
Return to Dragonshill
(#1502)

Margaret Way

Margaret Way
King Country (#1470)
Blaze of Silk (#1500)
The Man from Bahl Bahla
(#1530)

40 magnificent Omnibus volumes to choose from:

Essie Summers #1
Bride in Flight (#933)
Postscript to Yesterday
(#1119)
Meet on My Ground
(#1326)

Jean S. MacLeod
The Wolf of Heimra
(#990)
Summer Island (#1314)
Slave of the Wind
(#1339)

Eleanor Farnes
The Red Cliffs (#1335)
The Flight of the Swan
(#1280)
Sister of the
Housemaster (#975)

Susan Barrie #1
Marry a Stranger
(#1034)
Rose in the Bud (#1168)
The Marriage Wheel
(#1311)

Violet Winspear #1
Beloved Tyrant (#1032)
Court of the Veils
(#1267)
Palace of the Peacocks
(#1318)

Isobel Chace
The Saffron Sky
(#1250)
A Handful of Silver
(#1306)
The Damask Rose
(#1334)

Joyce Dingwell #1
Will You Surrender
(#1179)
A Taste for Love
(#1229)
The Feel of Silk (#1342)

Sara Seale
Queen of Hearts
(#1324)
Penny Plain (#1197)
Green Girl (#1045)

Jane Arbor
A Girl Named Smith
(#1000)
Kingfisher Tide (#950)
The Cypress Garden
(#1336)

Anne Weale
The Sea Waif (#1123)
The Feast of Sara
(#1007)
Doctor in Malaya (#914)

Essie Summers #2
His Serene Miss Smith
(#1093)
The Master to Tawhai
(#910)
A Place Called Paradise
(#1156)

Catherine Airlie
Doctor Overboard
(#979)
Nobody's Child (#1258)
A Wind Sighing (#1328)

Violet Winspear #2
Bride's Dilemma
(#1008)
Tender Is the Tyrant
(#1208)
The Dangerous Delight
(#1344)

Kathryn Blair
Doctor Westland (#954)
Battle of Love (#1038)
Flowering Wilderness
(#1148)

Rosalind Brett
The Girl at White Drift
(#1101)
Winds of Enchantment
(#1176)
Brittle Bondage (#1319)

Rose Burghley
Man of Destiny (#960)
The Sweet Surrender
(#1023)
The Bay of Moonlight
(#1245)

Iris Danbury
Rendezvous in Lisbon
(#1178)
Doctor at Villa Ronda
(#1257)
Hotel Belvedere (#1331)

Amanda Doyle
A Change for Clancy
(#1085)
Play the Tune Softly
(#1116)
A Mist in Glen Torran
(#1308)

Great value in Reading!
Use the handy order form

Complete and mail this coupon today!